SAVING THE PLANET
& STUFF

SAVING the PLANET & STUFF

GAIL GAUTHIER

G. P. Putnam's Sons ▪ New York

Library of Congress Cataloging-in-Publication Data
Gauthier, Gail, 1953– Saving the planet and stuff / Gail Gauthier. p. cm.
Summary: After losing his summer job with his uncle, sixteen-year-old
Michael agrees to go to work for an environmentalist magazine in Vermont
run by friends of his grandparents. [1. Summer employment—Fiction.
2. Environmentalists—Fiction. 3. Periodicals—Publishing—Fiction.
4. Interpersonal relations—Fiction.] I. Title. PZ7.G23435 Sav 2003
[Fic]—dc21 2002067954 ISBN 0-399-23761-5
1 3 5 7 9 10 8 6 4 2
First Impression

For Ian, Rob, and Will—
Saving the Planet's first editors

ONE

Michael Racine clutched his cell phone to his ear and began whispering into it just as soon as he heard a receiver being lifted at the other end of the line.

"What were you thinking of, letting me get into a car with Walt and Nora?"

His voice was as shrill and frantic as it was possible for a sixteen-year-old male's to be while trying to keep from being heard in an adjoining room.

"Hello?" a woman's voice said two states away in Connecticut.

"Mom! It's me. Michael Peter Racine the Third? The son you dropped off in front of his grandparents' house this morning with hardly more than a good-bye because you were late for work? The son whose own grandparents put him into a car with people they hadn't seen in, oh, I don't know, the better part of forty years? The son who's not supposed to be home again for weeks? Maybe never? Who knows?"

"Hello, sweetheart. I had trouble recognizing your voice.

You need to speak up and slow down. Are you enjoying yourself?" Ms. Racine asked. "Are Walt and Nora as nice as you thought they were going to be?"

"What do we actually know about Walt and Nora?" Michael demanded after looking over his shoulder to make sure the subjects of his conversation weren't near the door to the little study where he was placing his call.

"I believe I asked something very much like that last night," Ms. Racine said.

"You practically require references from kids I've known all my life before you'll let me go to the mall with them, but you let me go to another state with strangers! *Strangers!*" Michael wailed.

"Did something happen?" his mother asked anxiously.

By "something" his mother, a claims adjustor for an insurance company, didn't mean the kind of "something" anyone else would mean. "Well, I wasn't involved in any pileups on the interstate or shootings at a restaurant," he admitted. "No floods or fires or anything."

"You insisted on going with them," Ms. Racine reminded him. She was sounding less sympathetic now. It took death, dismemberment, natural disasters, or the occasional mutated gene going about its deadly disease-making business to arouse much in the way of compassion in her.

"I insist on lots of things. Why did you have to let me do this one?"

"So you've changed your mind about working in Vermont

for a few weeks for your grandmother's friends?" Ms. Racine asked.

Of course I've changed my mind! Michael wanted to shout. Come get me, Mommy! He just had to think of the right way to phrase it. And he had to think of it fast.

He carried the phone as far from the door as he could before saying into it, "Walt and Nora are weird, Mom."

"I believe your grandfather said something very much like that last night," Ms. Racine said.

"But I didn't know he meant *weird* weird. I thought he just meant *he didn't like them* weird. And let's face it, Mom; the list of things Poppy thinks is weird just because he doesn't like them goes on and on. Brands of deodorant, frozen foods, politicians, breeds of dogs . . . all kinds of stuff are on it."

"And what kind of weird are you talking about?" Ms. Racine asked.

"They don't believe in air-conditioning. I don't mean they don't believe there is such a thing. I mean they don't believe in using it. In spite of the fact that it's the end of July, I wasn't allowed to turn on the car's air conditioner because running an air conditioner requires extra energy from a car, and that cuts down on the number of miles you can get to a gallon of gas, so—"

"You're complaining because they're environmentalists?" Ms. Racine broke in. "I thought for sure you were going to say something about the old lady not wearing a bra."

"Ah, Mom, please!" Michael gasped.

"Well, if you had listened to your grandfather when he called last night and tried to talk you out of accepting their invitation instead of just holding the telephone receiver between your shoulder and your ear while you packed the CDs you were going to take with you for the trip, maybe you would have made a more informed decision."

Michael dropped a CD he'd been examining back onto a pile next to a stack of stereo equipment and pulled his phone from between his shoulder and ear.

"Poppy was talking about Nora's bra last night?" he asked in disbelief. Then a thought occurred to him. "How would *he* know whether or not she wears one?"

Ms. Racine sighed. "He said he knows all about her kind. He claims it's a political thing with her sort. He says she does it to make a statement showing her 'support,' if you'll excuse the pun, for the feminist movement. She's *not* a young woman, as I'm sure you've noticed. Maybe she should try to say something else. Of course, your grandfather could be wrong. What do you think?"

"About what?"

"About whether or not Nora wears a bra."

"Stop it!" he shouted into the phone, not caring who heard him. "Don't ever talk to me about this again!"

"Well, sweetheart, you kind of brought up the subject when you said they were weird. How was the trip?"

Michael perked up. Now was his chance to get the conversation going the way he wanted it to.

"The trip was wonderful," he said innocently. "I drove almost all the way."

"What do you mean? Didn't you take the interstate? You've only had your license a few months. You've hardly ever driven on the interstate."

Michael smiled. "There's nothing to it. And I can use a standard transmission now, too."

"You learned to drive a standard transmission on an interstate? What were you thinking of, driving that car?" his mother demanded.

"Well," Michael said, "I was thinking that Walt was going to kill me because he was doing fifty in the middle lane in a Volvo so old it must be a collector's item, while he had his right eye shut due to this peripheral-vision problem he has. Evidently it makes anything he sees from the right blurry and that bothers him, so when it happens, he just shuts his eye. We'd been going along like that for forty-five minutes before I noticed. It explained why we kept wandering into the right lane—he didn't know where the right lane was. So I offered to drive. Actually, I begged him to let me drive. Walt said the standard transmission wouldn't be a problem because I wouldn't have to shift so long as I didn't slow down or speed up. I was afraid to go less than fifty on an interstate, and he wouldn't let me speed up because the faster a car goes, the fewer miles to a gallon of gas it gets, and the fewer miles you're getting to a gallon of gas, the more gas you have to use, and poor gas mileage is going to cause civilization to fall. He just couldn't say enough about it. So . . ."

"I don't care about poor gas mileage or the fall of civilization," Ms. Racine said impatiently.

"I told him that," Michael replied. "I told him Dad didn't care, either. I told him—"

"Why didn't Nora drive if Walt was having problems?" Ms. Racine asked.

"She hasn't had a driver's license since 1981 or '82. She can't remember which year it was, but she's sure it was May, because her lilacs were in bloom. She actually went to the Department of Motor Vehicles and turned in her license because she no longer wanted to be responsible for pumping poisons into the Earth's lungs. 'We're of the Earth,' Nora says, 'so when we destroy her, it's like having a death wish,' and she has a strong will to live . . . Nora, not the Earth. I don't know why the Earth is always referred to as a she. Not that it should be called *he*, either. It should be called *it*, and—"

"Okay, I get it. Well, you made it up there, so I guess no harm was done." Ms. Racine sighed.

Damn, Michael thought. That didn't go well.

"Somehow I got the impression that Walt was going to be a fun guy," he complained. "But believe me, it was not fun having to listen to him drone on and on about this solid-waste crisis that I'd never even heard of and the number of pollutants emitted by gas-powered lawn mowers. It was like being with Poppy, if Poppy cared about solid waste, which he doesn't. What is it with old men? Walt did flip off a bunch of truck drivers who were working for companies he doesn't approve of, though. That would have been fun if I hadn't had to concentrate so hard on staying on the road. And then Nora got going on fluoride for some reason. She says the Chinese believe it lowers IQ, and then there's been some kind of study with rats' brains . . ."

"Your grandmother says they live their values," Ms. Racine said. "Some people like to talk about saving the planet. This Walt and Nora supposedly live their lives in such a way as to actually do it. You did bring your own toothpaste, didn't you? You know your father believes fluoride was one of God's greatest gifts to mankind, and if they don't use it—"

Michael had already heard all he wanted to about fluoride. "I wish Gram had warned me about this 'living your values' thing," he broke in. "You know Walt and Nora don't eat meat, right? I forgot about that when I said I would come stay with them. You should have seen where they made me eat lunch. Soy burgers were the best thing on the menu, and the waitress said they were out of them. The special was grilled mushrooms on onion focaccia bread. Who thinks of these things?"

"Listen, Mikey, I'll send you some money, and you can take the bus home," Ms. Racine offered.

Michael rolled his eyes heavenward. Victory at last.

"But what will you be doing once you come home?" Ms. Racine asked, as if she'd just thought of it. "You won't have a job. The job was in Vermont. That's why you went there."

There was a pause before Michael replied, "Stuff."

"You know what I'd like you to do when you get back? I'd like you to help your brother get ready for Boy Scout camp. It's going to be his first time there, and I think he's worried."

"He should be worried. He should be *very* worried."

"Why?" Ms. Racine asked. "You loved Boy Scout camp when you were his age."

"I wasn't Eddie. Mom, the kid's just out of grade school, and he's already memorized the periodic table of elements. There are some things that just shouldn't be done. Eddie scares people. A *gay* Scout would get along better in camp than Eddie will."

"Then he's lucky he's got you to help him. You know what else you can do? You can help drive Eddie to science camp. I hate having to ask Andrew's mother to do it all the time," Ms. Racine said. "He also has a chance to take part in a theater project at the middle school before he leaves for Boy Scout camp, and if you're here, you can drive me to work and then take him to the school so he can be in the play."

You watch, Michael told himself. His Royal Heinieness, Prince Eddie, will end up being the star of the show. Wait. Weren't we talking about my problem? How did this get to be about him?

"You got a postcard today," Ms. Racine said. "Do you want me to read it to you, or do you want to wait until you get home in a couple of days and read it yourself?"

Stay here or go home. Don't I have any other options? Michael asked himself.

"Oh, go ahead and read it to me," he said, none too eagerly.

"Just a minute. Okay, I've got it. It's from Marc. He's in Spain," Ms. Racine announced.

"Oh, great. I've been waiting to hear from him."

"It starts out, 'MP3.' That's so cute the way all your friends write your name like that. You know, Michael Peter the Third?"

"I get it, Mom."

Ms. Racine began to read aloud, *"MP3, I saw the Goya painting shown on the other side of this thing at the Museo de Prado yesterday. There's a girl from Italy who knows a lot about art history in our group. She speaks Spanish with an Italian accent and no French or English, but we communicate with an international language. Ha Ha Ha."*

Ms. Racine stopped reading long enough to say, "It's difficult to believe that Marc is an honor student in French and Spanish . . . or in anything at all, for that matter."

"Is that all he wrote?" Michael asked.

"There's another paragraph.

"Too bad about you losing that job with your uncle. Don't feel bad. A lot of famous people were fired from jobs when they were young. But your own uncle? Ouch. Marc."

"I can't believe it! *Everybody* thinks Uncle Bobby fired me!" Michael wailed. "How does a story like that get started?"

"And how did it get all the way to Spain?" Ms. Racine asked. "Oh, well. Tomorrow is Thursday. I'll put a check in the mail for you first thing in the morning. As soon as you get it, cash it and buy yourself a bus ticket. You could be home by Saturday night. Sunday at the latest. I'm going to arrange for the office to provide me with a car during working hours so you can have ours next week. Then you can drive Eddie and Andrew to science camp every day and give Andrew's mother a break."

"You know, maybe I should stay here. For a while, anyway.

They offered me a job, after all. It would be so rude for me to just take off. I can't very well tell them that I'm leaving because they belong on the Sci Fi Channel. But you can go ahead and send me money. Don't let me stop you."

"You sure? What's their house like? Is it okay?"

"It's some kind of solar building," Michael explained. "It seems more like a barn than a house, if you ask me. One side has hardly any windows and no doors. The other side is all glass, so anyone can see in. It looks like one of those big wooden dollhouses that are open on one side. It makes me feel as if some giant kid is going to reach in and get me."

"Did you get some dinner yet? They fed you, didn't they?"

"We had some chicken parmigiana that was in their freezer."

"Chicken?" Ms. Racine repeated. "I thought they were vegetarians."

"Uh-oh. If it wasn't chicken, what was it?" Michael asked.

After saying good-bye to his mother, Michael stood alone in the little room and stared at a blank computer screen. How did I get myself into this mess? he wondered.

Two

Just yesterday morning Michael had been sitting in front of his own computer in his own room, updating his "Rock Bands That Don't Suck" Web site. Except he hadn't been updating it because he'd updated it the night before, and that morning there was just nothing left to do to it.

So really he was just sitting in front of his computer. That's when he heard from Jonathan Blake. This was the first year they hadn't spent most of the summer hanging together. When Michael heard the chiming noise that signaled the arrival of an instant message on a computer screen, it had to be one of life's most beautiful sounds.

ProfBlakie: What's up?
MP3: thank god I've been on instant messenger for an hour&a half & you're the first sign of life I've found. I thought there'd been some natural disaster and I was the last of my kind left. how will I rebuild the human race? I kept wondering. what if the last woman on earth has been

irradiated somehow and has weird little wrinkly things growing out of her nose and forehead like on star trek? what if . . .

ProfBlakie: I get it.

MP3: I have 15 screen names on my buddy list you'd have thought somebody would have been on-line in the last couple of hours.

ProfBlakie: I have 32 names on my list but I only really talk with 12 of them.

MP3: oh

MP3: why aren't you digging for dinos today?

ProfBlakie: It's not even 8 am yet in this part of North Dakota.

Wow, Michael thought. Jonathan has a job so far away from home that he's in a different time zone. I've never been in a different time zone. I've only been as far as . . .

ProfBlakie: Too bad about you getting fired from that job. Talk about ruining your summer—stuck at home with squat for spending money.

Michael stared at the monitor with his mouth open. Then he frantically began to type.

MP3: I WASN'T FIRED!!! I was working for my uncle. what kind of jerk can't keep a job working for his own uncle?

ProfBlakie: Well, ah, you, I thought.

MP3: who told you I was fired? everyone we know is out of town.

ProfBlakie: My mother.

MP3: !!!! and she believed it? after all those years i spent drinking her soda & eating her potato chips she'd believe a story like that? about me?

ProfBlakie: I think she believed it BECAUSE of all those years you drank her soda and ate her potato chips.

MP3: I WASN'T FIRED!!! the job ended. that's entirely different.

ProfBlakie: Okay.

MP3: it's true! word got around that uncle bobby's landscaping business wasn't in good shape and no one wanted to hire him so there was no work for anyone who worked for him.

ProfBlakie: Why wasn't his business in good shape?

MP3: Uh. . . . he was passing bad checks.

ProfBlakie: Oops.

MP3: you should hear my brother. 'you mean you can get in trouble for not paying your bills?' if I live a hundred years I will never understand how Eddie got classified as gifted.

ProfBlakie: Clerical error. Those things stick with you for years.

MP3: so I wasn't fired.

ProfBlakie: Okay.

MP3: I wasn't

ProfBlakie: I thought it was strange. What would a person have to do to be fired from a job seeding and watering lawns? It's hard to imagine. You'll find something better. You'll have to! You won't find anything worse!

Michael scowled at his monitor. *I know that as high school summer jobs go, seeding and watering lawns for your uncle doesn't have anywhere near as much going for it as, say, serving an internship at a paleontological site in another time zone,* he thought. *But why does it have to be so obvious to everyone else?*

MP3: been out of work 1 week and I already have an interview for a job.
ProfBlakie: Whatever you do, don't go to the MickyD's down by Wal-Mart. The manager has a brutal body odor problem and no one can stand working there longer than a week.

Crap, Michael thought sadly. No wonder it had been so easy to get the interview.

ProfBlakie: I got a letter from Chris.

Chris was at a swanky art camp in Massachusetts where he'd scored a job just because he'd won dozens—maybe hundreds— of art competitions. Michael had written to him a whole two weeks earlier. Where was *his* letter?

MP3: his birthday was last week. 1st time since nursery school that he didn't have a party. bet he's sorry he left town now.
ProfBlakie: I got a postcard from Marc. He was in Spain.

Mine must have got lost in the mail, Michael told himself.

MP3: I saw Lindsey Grappo saturday. we might do
something later.

Which was entirely true. Lindsey was coming out of the library as Michael was going in to return books for his mother. She'd said, "How ya doin'?" and he'd replied by grunting at her. She was head lifeguard at the town's lake, probably because she was the tallest one there and had the best body. If I have a chance to do something with her later this summer or this year or this life, I am certainly going to jump at it, Michael promised himself.

ProfBlakie: Time for me to get to work. Bye.
MP3: Ya. I've got stuff to do too. See ya.

What? What stuff have you got to do? Michael asked himself as he stared once again at the Web site that really needed absolutely nothing done to it.

In nursery school Jonathan had had a case of separation anxiety so bad that he ran down the hall sobbing for his mother every morning for a month. It was Michael who sat with him in the block corner each day, knocking over piles of wood and laughing hysterically so Jonathan would think they were having a good time even though any fool could see they weren't. Chris couldn't look up at a teacher, let alone speak to one, for the first three years of school. It was Michael who, while they were in second grade, told Ms. Welling that Chris was going to puke, making it possible for him to get to the bathroom in time to toss his cookies instead of doing it all over his desk. And when Marc had become hysterical in kindergarten because he was spitting blood, it was Michael who reassured him by saying, "You've got a tooth ready to fall out, you idiot."

But oh, no, no one remembered any of that. It was all "What have you done lately, Mikey?"

I've done nothing, I'm doing nothing, and it looks as if I'm going to do nothing, Michael had to admit.

"Mikey! When are you getting off-line?"

"I don't know," Michael said automatically to his brother.

Eddie appeared in the doorway to Michael's room.

"My ride for science camp is coming soon, but first I have to get the requirements for the merit badges I'm working on at Boy Scout camp," Eddie explained.

"You aren't going to Boy Scout camp for weeks!"

"I don't like to wait until the last minute."

"The last minute is hundreds—maybe thousands—of minutes away. Besides, it's your first year at camp. You're going to work on fingerprinting and leather craft badges. You can do it in your sleep," Michael assured him.

"What if I don't want to do fingerprinting and leather craft?" Eddie asked, his nose wrinkled.

"No one wants to do fingerprinting and leather craft," Michael said. "But that's what you do your first year at camp. Are you following me? You're going to have to be like everybody else for once. Surprise! It won't kill you."

Michael turned his attention back to his monitor and hoped his brother would go away. When was the Little Prince leaving for Boy Scout camp again? Oh, that was right. Not soon enough.

He smiled. He wished he could see Eddie at camp, being like everybody else. Eddie *not* showering. Eddie *not* brushing his teeth. Eddie *not* changing his underwear. Unfortunately, Michael hadn't signed up for Boy Scout camp this year so he could work for his uncle . . . well, that and because he'd have been the only sixteen-year-old there since every other guy his age on the entire planet was off somewhere else.

Eddie's ride to science camp arrived, and he left to go clone stuff, leaving Michael alone to concentrate on . . . nothing.

His job had stunk. He only got it because the boss was his uncle. He didn't even have that anymore. All his friends were gone for the summer. On top of that, if he didn't find another job, he was going to have to live until school started on the three weeks of salary he'd made working for Uncle Bobby. Except it was only two weeks of salary because Uncle Bobby's last check had bounced.

He turned and looked at the clock next to his bed. It was only ten o'clock on a Tuesday morning. He had maybe fourteen hours to fill before he could go back to bed.

Tomorrow I've got to start sleeping later, he decided.

But for now what could he do? He figured he'd watched television for nineteen hours over the last day and a half. He could listen to CDs for a while, but then what would he do for the hours and hours and hours that were left in the day?

I should do something . . . big . . . something . . . I'm down to my last black T-shirt. I could do my laundry, he thought. No, it should be something bigger than that . . . I should start my own company. Yeah. Or I should invent something. I should create a new kind of software that would . . . would what? Well, I should do something, Michael repeated.

He pulled out his cell phone and dialed the number of his grandparents' house at Rock Haven Estates. The pool at Rock Haven, a community of exclusive homes for grandparents who had made a bundle and didn't care who knew it, was the only place Michael could go where he was admired simply for having all his own teeth and 20/20 vision. If his grandmother answered, he would ask her to pick him up, and she was sure to say yes. Then he could hang out at the pool for a few hours and listen to CDs later in the day after he got home.

What would have happened if Poppy had answered that call? Michael wondered as he lingered in Walt and Nora's study, not eager to go out and face them. I would have hung up, Michael realized. And then Poppy would have used his *69 button to find out who'd called and he would have called me back and chewed me out for not having anything to do. And I wouldn't have gone to the pool and been humiliated by Ms. Blackburn, who can swim circles around me. Though she is a triathlete, and is it really that bad for a triathlete who is almost seventy years old to kick the ass of a sixteen-year-old who isn't a triathlete? Or a biathlete? Or an athlete of any kind?

"She really kicked your ass, didn't she, Mike?" an elderly man sitting at a round metal table had said as Michael finally stumbled out of the pool.

Michael recognized Mr. Poljacik's voice and turned to see him sitting in the shade of an umbrella that sheltered his table.

"I . . . I thought I was going to come over here and just . . . float on top of the water . . . for a while," Michael gasped as he sat down at Mr. Poljacik's table.

"How many laps did she make you swim?"

"I couldn't keep track."

"You're a good boy to go in there and train with her," Mr. Poljacik told him. "No one here will go in the pool when she's in it. And she's in it all the time, I might add."

Michael shook his head sadly. He wasn't going to science scholar/genius/whatever camp like Eddie because, being just a B student, he wasn't eligible. But he was a "good boy." He wasn't going all over Europe for six weeks the way Marc was because he hated studying Spanish, wouldn't dream of trying to learn French, and didn't want to be stuck on another continent with no one who would understand him when he wanted to talk on the phone. Thank God he was a "good boy." Take art classes the way Chris did? Apply for internships—and get them—the way Jonathan had? Who needs all that when you're a "good boy"?

A "good boy," Michael repeated to himself once more. How lame is that?

Mr. Poljacik was smiling at him. "You couldn't have shown up at a better time," he said.

Michael smiled back. He couldn't recall an instance when Mr. Poljacik hadn't been glad to see him.

"What's up? You need your car washed? An idea for a birthday present for one of your grandsons? You still having that problem opening attachments to your e-mail? You want me to look at it?"

"I am just bored this morning, and you are always good company," Mr. Poljacik explained.

Michael looked pleased for a moment. Then the smile left his face. "I think you're the only one who notices."

He looked down at the paper Mr. Poljacik had spread over the table and saw that he had been reading the business section. "You got any hot tips?"

"What have I told you, over and over again? The Street is not a horse race. It is a scientific endeavor."

Uh-oh. Mr. P. wasn't going to quiz him on the definition of *price-earnings ratio* again, was he? Michael could never remember what that was.

And what if he asks me what *yield* means? What *does* yield mean? Michael wondered.

"Well, then, scientifically speaking, what do you think looks good?" Michael said.

"Technology is low right now," was all Mr. Poljacik would say.

"Is that good or bad?"

"Could be good. Could be bad."

"I read an article in a magazine that said there's a lot of development going on right now on drugs for sex problems. Maybe a pharmaceutical company would be a good investment," Michael suggested.

Mr. Poljacik looked up from the paper at Michael through his big, black-framed glasses. "That would depend on just how many people there are in the world with sex problems."

"I don't have any," Michael said quickly.

"Me, neither."

They were interrupted by a full-figured woman in a striped jersey and mint green shorts who was approaching their table. "Hey, Jeff, you got any hot tips?"

"Franny, if I've told you once, I've told you a hundred times. . . . The Street is not a horse race—"

"It is a scientific endeavor," Michael and Franny recited with Mr. Poljacik.

"Who's visiting your grandparents?" Franny asked Michael as she sat down with them.

"I didn't hear anything about anybody coming," Michael said.

"An out-of-state car pulled into their driveway about forty minutes ago. It's still there. Drop-in guests from out of state— I hate that," Franny observed. She paused and inspected Michael's hair, which was still wet. "How's the bleach job holding up?"

"I should have waited until after I'd had my hair cut to dye it. I did it myself and didn't do a very good job, and then it was time for a haircut, and a lot of the blond hair was cut off. So now it's just the tips that are blond," Michael explained.

Franny nodded. "I like that look." Her eyes widened. "I just found out that my niece's daughter knows you," she said. Her voice sounded concerned, and the expression on her thin face with its loose, ruddy skin had become very serious. "I was so sorry to hear that you'd lost your job."

Michael gasped as if he had been punched in the gut.

Mr. Poljacik's jaw dropped. "Mike! You lost your job? What happened?"

"Ah . . . I didn't actually 'lose' the job. It just sort of . . . ended."

Mr. Poljacik nodded. "I know how that is."

"Really. I was working for my uncle. I can keep a job with my own uncle."

"It's all right, dear," Franny said. "You don't owe us an explanation."

"It's happened to lots of people, Michael," Mr. Poljacik assured him.

Franny nodded kindly. "Lots of people get fired."

"But not me!" Michael insisted.

The three of them sat and tried not to look at one another.

Abruptly, Franny said, "My niece's daughter is your age—Lindsey Grappo?"

"Oh!" Michael uttered the word and turned his head as if he'd taken a fist to the jaw. Lindsey thinks I was fired. And she's telling people about it.

"You know she's head lifeguard at the lake?"

"Yeah, I'd heard." As if there was anyone who hadn't.

Franny relaxed, happy to have a safe subject to discuss. "She plays soccer, too. Between you and me, she works too hard. She was on the honor roll all last year, and she's sports editor for the school newspaper."

I've slipped into a terrifying alternate universe, Michael decided. Back in the real world, another Michael is listening to my Franny talk about her sister's never-ending urinary tract problems while I'm trapped here listening to an evil Franny talk about all the reasons why girls like Lindsey Grappo will never say more than "How ya doin'?" to me.

"She's spending a week this summer working as a counselor at a camp for handicapped children. She's going as a volunteer, of course. And the boy she's dating! He's . . ."

. . . Brandon Hastings. The guy you hope will get it next in a teen slasher movie.

". . . advanced placement chemistry . . ."

I have to take chemistry next year. I'd forgotten about that. Damn.

". . . went to a national future problem solvers conference . . . president of the Latin Club, treasurer of the Student Council, a member of the Cultural Awareness Club and the Chamber Singers."

Yup. That Chamber Singers thing is the icing on the cake. It's the thing that makes Brandon just plain creepy and . . .

"Can you imagine what his yearbook entry is going to look like when he graduates? It's going to go on for a quarter of a page." Franny laughed.

There's going to be nothing under my picture in the yearbook, Michael thought. I stopped going to computer club after the third meeting.

He could feel panic beginning to overwhelm him. What can I do to get something under my yearbook picture? he wondered. Could I be one of the people who carry the banner in front of the band when it marches in parades? How do you get that job?

Michael Peter Racine III

Didn't do basketball. Didn't do soccer. Didn't do track. Didn't do wrestling. Didn't do yearbook. Didn't do newspaper. Didn't do Drama Club. Didn't do Chorus. Didn't do Latin, French, or Spanish Clubs. Didn't do Cultural Awareness Club. Didn't do Problem-Solving Club. Didn't do Student Council. Did Computer Club for three weeks. Didn't . . .

"Well, Mikey, I'm glad you're not like Lindsey or that boy she's seeing. You're such a pleasure to be with—so funny and relaxing. You don't need to tell anyone this, but that Lindsey always makes me feel that any time she spends with the rest of the family is wasted. Whenever she's around, there's always this feeling that she really has more important things to do than be with us."

Franny reached out and patted Michael's hand.

"You never make me feel that way. You want to play cards?"

That's because I *don't* have anything better to do than be with them, Michael thought glumly while continuing to hide out in the little study in Walt and Nora's house just a day after having that conversation with Franny. Maybe I'm not that nice a boy, either. A really "nice boy" wouldn't have barged in on his grandparents when they had company. A "nice boy" would have found a ride home with someone and left the ancestors alone. But I played hearts for two hours—I am so good at hearts—and how was I supposed to remember that Franny had seen a strange car in their yard after two hours? You would think I'd have noticed it in the driveway when I got there, though. My parents are right. I've got to start paying more attention.

For instance, after finally arriving at his grandparents' home once he'd tired of thrashing senior citizens at the card table, he called to his grandmother to let her know he was in the house. Then he rushed down the hall to the bathroom to change into dry clothes, since bathing suits weren't allowed on the new retirement furniture. He heard his grandfather in the living room, saying, "Now, my younger grandson, Eddie, has just finished sixth grade. He's already in an accelerated math program. That means he'll be able to take precalculus his junior year." However, Michael's response to that was not to wonder who his grandfather was talking to, but to laugh at the thought that anyone would want to take precalculus his junior year, or ever. On his way back through the house, he wasn't even curious enough to stop in the living room. He just called "Hi, Poppy" to his grandfather and went on to the kitchen.

The room was empty, but he could hear someone moving around in the dining room next to it.

"Gram!" he said as he opened the refrigerator door. "Is it okay if I look for something to eat? It's after one, and I'm starving."

"We had omelets for lunch. *Mushroom* omelets," his grandmother replied as she hurried out of the dining room. "Let me make you one."

She knows how? Michael thought in disbelief, unable to remember when his grandmother had done more than open a can while preparing a meal.

"That's all right. I'll just make myself a sandwich. I see you have some ham in there."

Gram was suddenly standing next to him in front of the open refrigerator. "How about some fruit and crackers? It wouldn't take long to fix that."

"Really, Gram, a sandwich is all I want," Michael said as he bent forward so he could poke around at the contents of the refrigerator. "Oh, look! You have some nice bloody roast bee—"

His grandmother's hand dropped onto his shoulder and gave it a little shake as she whispered a quick "Shh" into his ear.

"It seems so strange to hear someone calling you Gram, Patricia," a voice said behind them.

Gram stepped back and Michael turned and leaned around the open refrigerator door so he could see who had spoken. Someone was walking through the opening between the dining room and the kitchen. She paused so the sunlight pouring into the wall of windows in the dining room was behind her and seemed to create a halo-like border for her slender frame. She had lifted one of her hands up to the back of her head so she could do something with the sandy-colored braid that began there and hung down between her shoulder blades. She was wearing a simple solid-colored dress without sleeves so her well-developed arms were exposed.

"Nora, this is my grandson Michael Peter Racine the Third," Gram said. "Mikey, this is Nora Blake. She and her husband stopped by on their way home to Vermont. We knew them when your grandfather was doing his orthodontic residency in Vermont in the early sixties. We met them again last summer on Cape Cod. It was the first time we'd seen them in ages."

"Oh, um . . . how do you do?" Michael offered awkwardly as Nora stepped toward him with her right hand out for him to shake.

"Your father went to school with my son for a few years," Nora said. "In fact, your grandmother ran the cooperative nursery school they attended in East Branbury."

She kept her face, with its small, straight nose and tiny mouth, directed toward him as she asked, "What do you prefer to be called? Mikey? Michael?"

"It doesn't matter," Michael said.

Nora smiled as she withdrew her hand. "Of course it matters."

"Really. You can call me whatever you want to, Ms. Blake," Michael told her, grateful that her grip was nowhere near as well developed as her biceps.

Nora's eyes widened. "Oh, titles like Mr. and Ms. or Doctor and Professor are just status labels. Please. Call me Nora."

She laid her hands on the refrigerator door and gently pushed it shut. "Let me close this for you while you decide what you're going to eat. If the internal temperature of the refrigerator rises too much, the compressor will have to work harder than normal to bring it back down, which uses extra energy, of course."

"Nora!" a strange man's voice called from the living room.

She turned her head in the direction of the sound, another smile starting to form even as she moved. When she looked back at Michael and Gram, it covered her face and her eyes had lit up.

"I have to go see what he wants," she said as she started to move away.

Before she had time to leave the room, Gram had pulled Michael closer to her and brought her mouth next to his ear. "Nora is a vegetarian," she whispered. "The kind who thinks eating the flesh of any living creature is immoral."

"It doesn't bother me," Michael whispered back as he pulled open the refrigerator door again.

Gram put an arm around Michael's shoulders. "Can I buy you off with Pop-Tarts? I got them special for you."

"What kind?" Michael asked.

"Brown sugar—with icing."

"That sounds nourishing."

Gram took his face between her hands and gave him a kiss.

"What was that for?" Michael asked.

"Because I love you no matter what."

There was something about the "no matter what" that undermined the "I love you" part of that statement, in Michael's opinion. He consoled himself with a couple of extra Pop-Tarts.

"Ah, Mikey, we were just talking about whether or not it's worthwhile to take PSAT prep courses," Poppy said from where he was stationed in his favorite chair.

"Oh? Is someone thinking of taking one?" Michael asked with his mouth full.

"Someone *should*," Poppy replied, glaring at him.

"Walt," Gram said, firmly breaking into the conversation and changing its subject, "this is our grandson Michael Peter the *Third*." She gave Michael a squeeze. "Mikey, this is Nora's husband, Walt Marcello."

Michael was only of average height and weight, himself, so the big man lounging at one end of Gram's white love seat looked particularly huge to him. Walt Marcello sat with his legs crossed and one of his very old running shoes propped on the square coffee table that had once belonged to some dead relative and was as valuable as it was ugly. One of his knees had popped through his blue jeans—from the looks of it, sometime that morning. His worn T-shirt with its faded picture of either Karl Marx or Jerry Garcia (Michael couldn't tell which) was a far cry from his own grandfather's white jersey that was carefully tucked into the top of a pair of freshly ironed khaki pants. But his clothing was barely noteworthy compared with Walt's shoulder-length gray ponytail, pulled back from a *very* receding hairline, and the little gold hoops in each of his earlobes.

"Michael Peter the Third, huh?" Walt's thin lips contorted under his healthy-sized nose as he directed the question toward Poppy. "You have two orthodontists in this family and three people with the same name. You have trouble coming up with new ideas?"

Michael answered for his grandfather. "My younger brother is named Edmund. That's what they chose when they couldn't use Michael again. They are just not good with new ideas."

Walt grimaced in agreement.

"Eddie was named for a tenth-century prince," Gram explained.

"Prince Edmund Ironside!" Nora exclaimed. "Of course."

"Of course?" Michael repeated. "Of course? In twelve years you're the first person I've met who's heard of him. I thought my little brother was named for Eddie Munster until I was in the fourth grade."

"My daughter-in-law was a history major," Poppy explained.

"Whew. A little bit of education is a dangerous thing, isn't it?" Walt said.

Michael laughed. "At least he was named for a *prince*. You know, royalty and all. I was named for a line of *orthodontists.*"

Walt shrugged. "Things could be worse. Your folks could have named one of you Richard after that king who was known as the Lion-Hearted. Wouldn't that have been nice? To be named after someone so courageous, he was said to have the heart of a lion? But you know what people who are named Richard are called, don't you? *Dick.* Now, there's a label you wouldn't want to go through life with."

Michael stood, holding his plate of cooling Pop-Tarts, staring at Walt.

"Well, think about it."

Michael was thinking about it. He was thinking about how he had just heard a dick joke. A *dick* joke! In front of his grandparents! Both of them!

"I think it's time to raise the tone of this conversation," Poppy announced.

Oh, of course, Michael thought glumly as he found himself a place to sit on the raised hearth in front of the fireplace.

"I saw a good show on public television a few weeks ago," Walt offered.

"Did you? I really enjoy public television," Poppy said.

"We call it *pubic* television at school," Michael offered.

Poppy pounded the arm of his chair with one hand while raising the other one to point at Michael.

" 'Pubic television' . . . not bad," Walt said, nodding his head appreciatively.

"I didn't think of it myself," Michael admitted modestly.

"You and your friends watch much PBS?" Walt asked.

"I'm not even sure what channel it's on."

"You ought to find out. A couple of weeks ago I was watching one of their programs and all of a sudden I caught some breast shots . . . twice. Talk about your pleasant surprises. I'd been having trouble following the show's plot—it was one of those English stories about students at Oxford—but it kept my attention after that because that actress had quite a nice rack on her."

"I don't mind nudity so long as it isn't just female," Nora said. "When it's just women who are undressed, there's always a risk of exploitation. But this show Walt's talking about included a scene with a man naked from the back. That provided balance."

"Gee," Michael said, "I always thought that anyone who watched English shows on PBS had crossed the line into the Land of the Old Farts. But if they're showing topless actresses—"

"The old farts might be onto something, huh?" Walt suggested.

"Are you sure you weren't watching HBO?" Poppy asked impatiently.

Walt shook his head. "No. We don't get cable."

"We don't believe that the public's access to popular culture should be controlled by private companies," Nora explained. "The airwaves should be free."

"I never thought of it that way," Gram said. "That makes so much sense."

"Oh, Patty, it does not," Poppy snapped.

"This show you're talking about—do you suppose they'll be rerunning it sometime?" Michael asked Walt. "Sometime soon?"

"I'd like to tape it if they do," Walt said. He grinned at Poppy, leaned forward, and rested an elbow casually on one of his knees. "If I do manage to tape it, I'll send you a copy," he offered. "You can watch it with the kid, here. You know, sort of a shared cultural experience?"

"Gee, Poppy, we've never watched naked women together," Michael pointed out, grinning.

Annoyance rose out of Poppy like heat waves rippling up from hot pavement. It was *so* easy to get his grandfather going, sometimes Michael didn't even have to try. Often, in fact, he wasn't trying. It just happened. He couldn't help himself. Which sometimes took the fun out of it. There's no challenge anymore, Michael decided. I say something, he gets PO'ed. We're in a rut.

"I'm sorry, I didn't hear that," Michael had to say to Nora when she spoke to him.

"What are you doing this summer?" Nora repeated.

He looked at his grandfather. Poppy looked pleased, as if there was nothing he'd like more than to have the story of his grandson's summer dragged out in front of his friends.

"Nothing," Michael finally said.

Nora laughed. "That is such a classic answer. Young people always think they're doing nothing, but there's no such thing as doing nothing."

"You don't know Mikey," Poppy observed. "When he says he's doing nothing, he means he's doing nothing. He has a gift for it."

"Good for you, kid," Walt said.

"I had a job," Michael said, feeling defensive. "But . . ."

"It ended?" Nora suggested.

Michael stared at her in amazement. "That's *exactly* what happened! It ended!"

Nora tipped her head and considered Michael. "Hmmm. I bet now you're not doing 'nothing' at all. You just don't know what you're doing."

Poppy snorted. "That's probably it."

"Let's think about this another way," Nora suggested. "What do you want to do—not just this summer, but with your life?"

There was a long silence while Michael stared at her.

Nora patted his knee. "What are you good at doing?" she asked.

"Well . . . let's see . . . I'd have to say . . . nothing, actually," Michael said, trying to sound as if he were being very modest rather than just honest.

"Nonsense. Mikey is very good at checking his e-mail and talking with his friends on Instant Messenger," Poppy told Nora. "He just has to find somebody who will pay him to do that."

"Well, there you have it!" Nora exclaimed. "You could go into the field of communications."

The field of communications, Michael repeated to himself. Which is?

"And what would that be?" Poppy asked.

Nora smiled. "He'll find out."

"It's not like he doesn't have time," Walt said. "We were nearly thirty before we started the magazine. Who'd have thought we'd ever do something like that?"

"Not me," Poppy replied.

"Oh, Mike, what's wrong with you today?" Gram complained to her husband. She turned to Nora. "We were so excited when your magazine began getting so much attention and you both became so well known."

"We were stunned, really," Poppy broke in. "We were

stunned that two people such as yourselves who were damn near Communists with all your talk of redistributing wealth to the masses and saving the stinking planet were becoming rich and famous."

"I'm so sorry to disappoint you, Mike, but we share ownership of *The Earth's Wife* with our employees." Nora laughed.

"And Earth's Publications, our book publishing company, makes so little money that nobody wants to own part of it," Walt added. "Nora's had trouble finding time to give that as much attention as it needs."

"That's changing now that we have a managing editor for the original magazine," Nora said.

Michael suddenly realized to whom he'd been talking about dick jokes, breast shots, and his sorry excuse for a life. He looked toward his grandparents. "These are the . . . the . . . people . . . you know who run the magazine about . . ."

He had to stop there because he would have been very hard put to say what, exactly, the magazine he was thinking of was about, never having actually read one of them himself.

"About individuals celebrating and caring for our household, the Earth," Nora said helpfully.

"Freaks' Home Journal is how your grandfather referred to it once last summer," Walt said.

"Yes! Yes! That's the one!" Michael agreed eagerly. "You guys are famous, aren't you?"

"In some circles they are," Poppy agreed.

"The Earth's Wife is a very well regarded publication, Mikey. Nora and Walt started it themselves in 1968, and Nora's been

editing it for more than thirty years now," Gram said. "It's an alternative magazine. It covers things that a regular magazine might not be interested in—like those toxic waste sites you publicized years ago."

"Is it true," Michael asked, "that you print the magazine on newsprint instead of glossy pages because some of your readers are so into recycling that they use it for toilet paper and newsprint does the job better?"

Gram gasped, and Poppy groaned and looked embarrassed.

Whoops, Michael thought, watching Walt straighten and half turn toward Nora as if looking for some kind of signal from her. How could I have known? It had sounded . . . well, not reasonable, but possible . . . when Poppy had said it.

Then Nora started to twitch. Her chest and shoulders rose in a sort of rhythm, and laughter began to bubble up toward her head. She put one hand up to her mouth as if trying to keep it from spilling out.

"He has to have heard that from you, Mike. You were always so funny," she gasped.

Walt relaxed against the back of the couch.

"You're the one with a good sense of humor, Nora," Poppy said graciously.

"I'm . . . uh . . . sorry, if I embarrassed anyone," Michael said awkwardly.

" 'If'?" Poppy repeated. " 'If'? How can you not know?"

"I know," Michael muttered miserably.

Nora got up from the couch and was suddenly leaning over Michael, her long, warm fingers clasping both his hands. Her face was level with his and she was smiling and saying, "We all had a good laugh. Don't give it a thought," as if she wasn't just being polite, but really meant it. Then her hands slipped off his, and she sort of flowed back to her seat, leaving Michael feeling that everything actually was okay. Right that second, everything was actually good.

"I've heard my parents talk about you, not just Poppy," he said eagerly as Nora settled herself in her chair. "This is so cool. Here I am, right here with people who have their own magazine. I have all these friends from school who are doing these neat things this summer like working at art camps and on paleontological digs. I can't wait to tell them I just *found* magazine publishers in my grandparents' living room."

"I know just what you mean about your friends," Nora told him. "We just came from visiting both our children. This is the first year that none of our grandchildren have come back with us. One of them is a competitive gymnast, so he's at some special camp, training, and another one has started some special college program where she studies writing in the summer. Then there's the musician—he's playing with a couple of youth orchestras, so he can't spend any time with us."

Michael and Nora stared sadly at each other.

"It does seem as if most kids have something to do, doesn't it?" Poppy said, giving Michael a meaningful look.

"Just the dumb ones," Michael snapped. "The smart ones figure a way to do nothing. Not that I want to . . . uh . . . make out that your grandchildren are dumb or anything," he quickly added to Nora.

"I could tell you didn't mean anything like that," Nora assured him.

"Hey, kid, you don't have anything to do, and we don't have anybody to do anything with. You want to come on back to Vermont with us?" Walt asked.

"Uh," Michael said, unenthusiastically.

"We'll find something for you to do at the magazine," Walt suggested.

Michael couldn't believe what was happening. A job with a magazine! And staying with a woman who actually understood about jobs just ending! And a man who knew how to find naked women on PBS! How did all that compare with working at an art camp or traveling for six weeks in countries that didn't offer American television? Damn well, Michael realized.

"Oh, Patricia, I would love to have your grandchild with me for a few weeks," Nora said.

"I think it would be wonderful for Michael," Gram said.

Poppy caught Michael's eye and shook his head at him. He mouthed the words "say no" several times.

"Going to Vermont sounds great!" Michael exclaimed.

Just twenty-four hours later, Michael took a deep breath and prepared to finally leave the study and go out into Walt and Nora's living room. I probably would have thought a trip on the *Titanic* sounded good, too, he thought sadly.

THREE

Michael had described Walt and Nora's home, with its glass wall to let in the heat of the sun and solar collectors stationed on the roof, as being like a large doll's house. That was particularly true of the long room downstairs that ran the length of the building.

"Make yourself comfortable," Nora called to him from the kitchen at the other end of the house, where she and Walt were finishing cleaning up after dinner when he came out of the study. "We're almost done here."

He sat down on one of the two brown couches that were stationed on either side of a coffee table covered with magazines as well as the two weeks' worth of mail and newspapers they'd picked up at the post office on their way through town. All that kept the whole world from being able to peer in at him through the wall of glass on the southern side of the house was a nearly empty greenhouse built right against it.

He turned to look over the back of the couch toward his

hosts, started to speak, stopped, started again, and stopped again. Finally, he blurted out, "What did we have for dinner?"

"Eggplant parmigiana. I've heard that when eggplant is fried in a good thick breading, like the one Walt uses, it can be mistaken for chicken. What did you think?" Nora asked as she walked toward him.

Michael gagged.

"Are you okay? You sure?" Nora asked as she sat down next to him.

"I think I was choking on something," Michael explained. Yeah, something like eggplant, he added to himself. I'm going to starve here.

"I can't tell you how impressed I am with the way you jumped at the chance to do something new and different and came to a strange place with people you hadn't even known twenty-four hours," Nora said.

"Impressed" isn't the word I'd use, Michael thought.

Nora sighed and shook her head. "Change—it's like a life force. It's the avenue to every opportunity. But so few people are able to embrace it. Your ability to do that is a gift. Be careful to nurture it."

Michael beamed in the glow of all Nora's compliments and thought, What?

"When I was young, I so wanted to be like you. I wanted to be spontaneous," she explained. "But spontaneity was a real effort for me. I had to work at it."

She threw her head back and laughed. Fine lines rippled

away from her mouth and nose in both directions across her pale skin. Her hair, Michael noticed, wasn't sandy at all, the way he'd thought the day before. It was that faded, washed-out color you see on redheads when they were . . . old.

"If you have to work at it, than I guess you're not being spontaneous, are you?" she said when she noticed Michael was just staring and smiling at her.

"Uh, I guess not," Michael said distractedly as he struggled to keep his eyes from drifting down below her shoulders.

"We're going to put you in our younger son's old bedroom. I'm sorry it's such a mess. We've been storing some things up there, and we weren't expecting company. But you'll have the whole upstairs to yourself and your own bathroom, so it will be private. Are your eyes bothering you?"

Michael had been blinking them rapidly, hoping that would keep Nora from noticing that they kept darting down to her chest.

Does she wear a bra? Michael wondered. She just got through saying all those nice things about me (at least they sounded nice), and all I want to do is stare at her . . . Oh, cripe. Now I'm turning into some kind of pervert.

"I think . . . uh . . . I'm having some kind of pollen problem," he managed to say.

"I'll get you a cold, damp cloth to put on them," Nora said as she stood up. "Then I'll go upstairs and put clean sheets on that bed."

Nora walked away from him, past the freestanding, metal

fireplace against the wall, opposite the greenhouse, that separated them from the study and a master bedroom, past the dining area, and into the bathroom next to the kitchen. Michael
collapsed against the back of the couch, relieved to have her
bra area out of his line of vision.

He gasped as Walt shouted at Nora's retreating figure,
"There's going to be a spot opening up on the Planning and
Zoning Board. You think I have a chance of being elected if I
run for that seat this fall?"

Michael had forgotten about him. Walt had opened the slid-
ers into the greenhouse and moved a wooden rocking chair
into the opening so he was right across from the couches. He
was wearing a pair of half glasses while he read the newspaper.
Sitting there in the rocker like that, he looked somewhat worn
down, the way statues are worn down by rain . . . wind . . .
whatever. The bones in Walt's cheeks and shoulders seemed
more prominent than they should be. The flesh that had once
covered them seemed to have dropped a bit, as if gravity was
pulling everything south.

Why do my grandparents know such old people? Michael
wondered. Oh. That's right. My grandparents *are* old people.

"If enough people have forgotten what it was like the last
time you were a P and Z Board member, sure," Nora said as she
came back with a wet cloth. She grinned as she handed it to
Michael and shoved a few things to one side on the coffee table
so she could sit down on it. "It's been what—twenty years? A
lot of people have died and moved out of town since then. Go
for it, Walt."

Michael rubbed the cloth quickly across his eyes and then took another swipe at them, hoping that would be enough to make Nora feel she hadn't wasted her time getting it.

"A lot of folks appreciate what I did for this town," Walt grumbled as he flipped a page.

Michael looked down at the worn barn-board coffee table Nora was seated on. Next to her were old copies of *The Journal of Edible Weeds, The Bulletin of Ecologically Safe Transportation Methods,* and *Sustaining Life on the Home World.* Michael didn't think he'd be doing any reading anytime soon, and since there was no sign of the television remote control, he didn't have to keep himself busy fighting the temptation to rudely turn on the TV right in the middle of someone else's conversation. He looked over at Walt and, for want of anything else to do, said to him, "So, what *did* you do for this town?"

"I stopped a mall from coming here, for one thing," Walt said while studying something in his paper.

"Really?"

"Pretty much by himself," Nora added. "The plan had a lot of support."

"That was good, clean fun," Walt sighed. Then he looked up at Michael. "Haven't I heard your pappy owns a mall, kid?"

" 'Poppy.' He owns two office buildings and part of an enclosed mall. Investment properties. Bothering the building managers gives him something to do now that he's retired," Michael explained. "The mall's a nice one, too."

"There's no such thing as a nice mall," Walt said as he looked back at his newspaper.

"I've been to some terrific malls when we've been on vacation. Huge ones."

Walt dropped the newspaper onto his lap, took his glasses off, and looked across the room at Michael. "You go to malls while you're on vacation?"

The indignation in Walt's voice brought a grin to Michael's face. "Sure. Doesn't everybody?"

"You *shop* while you're on vacation?" Walt asked, sounding horrified.

Mostly they just walked around in malls in the evenings or on rainy days, but Walt's reaction was more than Michael could resist. Air conditioners, sixty-five-mile-an-hour speed limits, malls . . . was there anything that *didn't* tick this guy off?

"Well, sure," he told Walt. "What if Abercrombie & Fitch runs a sale and you're out of town? That's the beauty of malls. They have the same stores all over the country. You never miss a thing."

Walt laughed, shook his head, and appeared ready to go back to reading his paper. Michael, however, didn't give up easily.

"So, what do you guys do while you're on vacation?" he asked just to try to keep the conversation going.

"Now our vacations are usually planned around visiting our grandchildren," Nora explained for Walt. "But when our sons were living with us, we used to do things like stay on a farm for a couple of weeks and work with the farmer and her family. Once we stayed on an island that could only be reached by boat. That was a great vacation. Let's see. What other things did we do? Well, one summer we went out west and volunteered at a school on a Native American reservation. Then there was the year we did a tour of the birthplaces of our favorite authors—Henry David Thoreau . . . Rachel Carson . . . Wendell Berry—have you read any of their work, Michael?"

Since Michael never remembered authors' names, he could truthfully say, "I don't know. Maybe . . ."

"They're nature writers," Walt said, his voice indicating he wasn't taken in by Michael's evasiveness. "I'm sure we've got some copies of their books around here somewhere. If you read a few chapters, maybe it would refresh your memory."

"We took turns reading them out loud in the car that year," Nora recalled, smiling. "That was another great trip."

Michael tried to picture the scene: Younger versions of Walt and Nora would be sitting in the front of a car, probably the same car they still drove, with a couple of kids comatose from boredom in the backseat while Nora read from a *very* thick book.

"The buttercups in the meadow were my only neighbors. And fine neighbors they were! Sometimes, while visiting with an acquaintance in the polluted, nasty town, I have thought of my old friends the buttercups and longed to be with them. They never have a harsh word to say of another, be he buttercup or man, nor do they take from another, living totally on what they get from the sky—sun and rain. And perhaps some nutrients from the earth. Oh, but if only we could be as simple as the buttercups."

I'm definitely going to start treating my parents better, Michael promised himself. They're nowhere near as bad as they could be.

"We had a good vacation this year," he said. "At the end of June we did a tour of three different Six Flags Theme Parks. We took turns reading the brochures out loud in the car so we could decide what attractions to go to first. You have to get to the best rides early in the day, before the lines get too long." Michael looked over at Walt. "There was an outlet mall near one of the parks. A big one."

"Outlets!" Walt repeated in a tone of voice that suggested he would have spit after he said the word if only he'd been outside. "When we were on vacation, we did things that involved *experiencing* something. We got away from our own lives and lived something entirely different. That's what a vacation is supposed to be. It's not supposed to be another opportunity to shop, which you can do absolutely anywhere."

Michael tried to look thoughtful, as if he were giving what Walt had just told him a great deal of consideration, and then said, "Isn't everything an experience? In which case, shopping would be an experience, too? And if you're shopping for something you've never owned before, you'd be living a really new experience, something entirely different. Hence, shopping is a fine vacation activity."

Walt threw his newspaper down on the floor and stood up. " 'Hence' it is not," he said abruptly to Michael.

Then he turned to Nora. "I'm going on-line for a while," he announced.

Michael jumped up and started to follow him out of the room. "You have Internet access? Great! I haven't checked my e-mail all da—"

Walt turned around and glared. "I haven't checked my e-mail in a couple of weeks."

"I didn't think people your age got e-mail," Michael said. As the words slipped out of his mouth, he realized they might be just a little rude for a new houseguest.

Walt's eyes grew large and he straightened up, making himself look even larger, the way some animals are said to do when trying to frighten off a predator. "And what is that supposed to mean?"

Oh, yeah, Michael thought, I went too far. Now what do I do?

"Uh . . . what do *you* mean?" he asked, trying to buy some time.

"You really enjoy pissing people off, don't you?" Walt said to him.

"You really shouldn't be criticizing others about pissing people off, Walt," Nora pointed out.

"Oh, I'm not being critical," Walt insisted. "That was the thing I liked about you, kid. When you were all over Puppy yesterday—that made a very nice impression on me. But let's get something straight. I like it when you piss *other* people off. I don't like it when you piss *me* off. Understand?"

I could just nod my head and this will be over, Michael realized. But he didn't.

"I'm not sure," he said instead. "Are you saying you'd like me to piss other people off for your pleasure?"

"I hadn't thought of that, but yes, that's a good idea. Right now, though, what I want is for you to shut up. Disappear, even," Walt explained. "Can you do that?"

"Like, into thin air or something?" Michael asked, determined to get in the last word.

But Walt seemed equally set on getting the upper hand by being the last one to speak. "Like moving your as—"

"Michael is going to go upstairs with me to see his room," Nora broke in. "You go do whatever you want to, Walt. Now. Go."

Walt turned on his heel, went into the study, and slammed the door.

"He really likes you," Nora said to Michael. "I could feel the positive vibrations."

"I thought I was feeling something, too," Michael agreed as he picked up his backpack and duffel bag and followed Nora.

There was no second story over the living-dining-kitchen area. There was open space above it, right up to the top of the building. But the other half of the house—the half that contained the study, master bedroom, and bathroom—had two bedrooms and a bathroom over it. They were a little smaller than the corresponding downstairs rooms because a balcony overlooking the open area served as a hallway. It was reached by a set of wide steps near the TV. A wooden railing ran from the bottom step up to the top and along the balcony.

Michael went up to the balcony after Nora, followed her past the bathroom to the second bedroom, and stopped in his tracks in the doorway.

There were two small, horizontal windows crammed between two narrow closets and above a set of built-in drawers on the exterior wall across from him ("Built-in furniture provides extra insulation," Nora explained). Michael barely noticed them because he was so busy taking in the bed, the floor of a closet—its door couldn't be shut—a little table with an arrangement of cobweb-draped dried flowers, and an armchair with a matching footstool, which were all covered with . . . stuff.

"I'm afraid we've collected a few things over the years," Nora said apologetically.

"Wow. You collect bags of Styrofoam beans," Michael said, pointing to four bags filled with them.

"They aren't biodegradable, so we didn't want to throw them out when the town still had a landfill. We use them as packing when we want to mail something," Nora explained.

Michael lifted a roll of used bubble packaging off from the bed. "I guess you don't mail stuff very often, huh?"

Nora took the roll from Michael. "I keep meaning to take them into the office. They'll get used there. Maybe we could bring them with us tomorrow."

The rest of the room's contents would not be as easy to dispose of. There were a couple of bundles of brown paper bags, and plastic sacks filled with more plastic sacks. There was a pile of very ratty bath towels, a half dozen decorative tins of various sizes, partially burned candles, empty cardboard boxes, a variety of canvas satchels stamped with the names of various organizations, two partial sets of dishes, stacks and stacks and stacks of magazines, three . . .

"You see," Nora began awkwardly, "we're trying to control

waste by diverting materials from landfills—which are reaching capacity in a lot of places, you know—and the regional incinerators that are replacing them. We did an article in *The Earth's Wife* on that in, I think, June of '98."

So they're diverting materials from the landfill to their spare bedroom? Michael wondered.

"Of course, it's not waste in the sense of filthy garbage. It's waste in the sense that these are all things that would be thrown away by most of America even though they can still be used. Look at these canvas bags. Some of them are brand-new. Isn't it awful the way people squander resources on elaborate promotional items like these that no one wants? It just makes me crazy to see that kind of thing."

Crazy, huh? Michael repeated to himself nervously.

"People use recycling as a crutch. They buy all kinds of junk, figuring they'll just recycle part of it after they're done. We at *The Earth's Wife* promote *pre*cycling. Don't buy it in the first place, and you won't have to worry about what to do with it afterward."

They need to promote the precycling thing a whole lot harder, Michael thought. It doesn't seem to be working here.

Nora swatted some plastic shopping bags filled with more plastic shopping bags off the bed and sat down in a heap. "I'd put you in the other room, but we keep all our bulk purchases in there, and those things are heavy. You use a lot less packaging when you buy in bulk. The last time we did an article on that was maybe '96 or '97." She sighed. "You can't imagine what I go through trying to get these rooms cleaned up before my daughters-in-law come to visit. Years ago you used to be able to sell some of these types of things at a tag sale. Not anymore."

Michael wasn't surprised. He wouldn't have believed anyone would have bought any of it, ever.

"Whenever we know the kids are coming, we start hauling the junk in the bedrooms down to the cellar. But most of that area is filled up with the tons of stone we need to store heat for the solar heating system, and then there's Walt's workshop and his copper collection."

"Walt has a copper collection?" Michael asked. "So does my grandmother. She collects copper pans and kettles and stuff. She keeps them in the kitchen, though, not the cellar."

"Oh. Well, Walt collects copper pipe. And wire. You can sell it!" Nora said defensively. "Over the course of fifteen to twenty years, you can collect enough copper to make maybe a hundred dollars. It takes up a little room, though. And what with all the things we've brought down to the cellar over the last few years, we can't get much more in there."

"So the cellar's as bad as this? Not that this is actually bad," Michael added in a rush. "I mean—"

"The cellar is worse, actually."

Michael whistled.

"I wish people would just think about the trash that's generated during one lifetime. And then when you multiply that by all the lifetimes on this planet in just one generation, it makes you wonder how we've managed to live here this long."

Michael silently wondered how long he'd manage to live in that room.

"You know what would be cool?" he finally said. "If you mounted some sort of Web cam in here. People could watch on the Internet as the garbage got deeper and deeper. You could really make a pile in here if you started throwing in trashier things from the kitchen. Oh, and the bathroom. I bet you could throw some nice ripe stuff in here from the bathroom. After I've gone back home, of course."

Nora smiled at him. "I'm interested in instructing, not entertaining."

Michael nodded. From what he'd heard of *The Earth's Wife*, that was all too true.

Suddenly, Nora's eyebrows shot up. "But you know what we *could* do? We could do a photo layout on this room and an article for *The Earth's Wife*." She jumped to her feet. "Yes! I'll have Roberta come out here tomorrow and take some shots. Then we'll do a story on all the different ways these things could be used instead of being wasted!" She started to run out of the room. "Walt!" she called before she turned back to Michael. "We call the monthly editorial 'The Earth's Wife in the Twenty-First Century.' There's an editorial I've been thinking about that would relate to this," she explained as she ran out the door.

She came back to the doorway. "The only thing is, we won't be able to start cleaning this room up for you until after the pictures are taken. We can unload the bed and put on clean sheets, but we'll have to leave everything heaped up around it. Is that okay? Do you mind terribly?"

"Can I be in some of the pictures?" Michael asked.

Nora gasped. "What a wonderful idea! Yes! Of course!"

Nora ran out of the room, calling for Walt again.

Michael looked around the room. He wondered if it could ever be cleaned up enough to make him want to unpack his ten CDs, his compact disc player, the three computer games he'd brought along just in case he'd have a chance to use them, the two books his father had forced him to pack that he had no intention of looking at let alone reading, his three pairs of sneakers, or his boxer shorts, socks, pants, and shirts. Or the hooded sweatshirt and gloves he'd added at the last minute because he was headed north to Vermont, and it was a well-known fact that Vermont had lots of cows and tractors and was colder than other places.

Those pictures, he told himself, will have to be really, really good to make up for having to sleep in all this.

FOUR

Michael did not have a good night.

His mother had investigated a few . . . dozens . . . hundreds of house fires and said that tons of them had been caused by homeowners who had crammed their houses full of all kinds of flammable items. Those boxes, magazines, towels, books, clothing—any *one* of the things they've got piled up in here will go up like a torch under the right conditions, he thought over and over again. What are the right conditions? What about the Styrofoam beans? Didn't Eddie do a science-fair project that proved Styrofoam didn't burn, it melted and emitted toxic gases? Or was that the upholstery in our living room furniture? The dishes they've got stacked on the floor somewhere won't burn, anyway. No, I'll just fall over them if I have to run for my life.

And the cellar. God only knew what was in the cellar. It was Michael's guess Walt and Nora sure didn't. The whole downstairs would be in flames by the time anyone knew there was a fire in the cellar. Film at eleven.

He lay rigid in his bed, listening and listening for the crackling sound he thought a fire would make. He'd doze off and then flinch on his sweaty sheet as he woke and wondered, What was that? And that? And that? Then he'd lay rigid for a while longer. Then he'd wonder if the house was hot like this because Walt and Nora had central air and refused to use it the way they refused to use the air conditioner in the car. Or was it hot because the cellar had turned into a giant barbecue pit? Then he'd doze off. Then he'd wake up. Then the cycle would start again.

That was how he spent the entire night until suddenly there was a flash of light, a whir, and he was gasping and moaning and struggling to find a clear space next to his bed so he could get down on his hands and knees and crawl through the smoke to the door.

"I scared you, didn't I?" a voice whispered above him. "I didn't mean to."

Michael whimpered and looked up at a woman holding a camera.

"Actually, I did mean to scare you," she said in a more normal voice. "Catching people unaware is my specialty. I frighten most of my subjects."

As Michael's head cleared, the figure before him slowly came into focus. The first things he noticed were the denim-covered thighs. *Thunder thighs* was the term that came to mind.

A gut stuck out from under the shirttail of a plaid cotton blouse. Cripe, hasn't she ever heard of ab videos? Michael wondered. A normal-looking torso (all things considered) led up to a long, slender neck. And at the end of the neck sat a round face with a look that suggested its owner was always just a little bit worried. The whole package was topped off with hair that had been dyed blond but not very well.

"A lot of my subjects aren't alive, of course. I shoot a lot of home decorating scenes, food, and outdoor pictures. But even with those I like to try to get a shot before the designers or the owners or whatever have everything just the way they want it. So if those things were capable of being surprised, I'd be surprising them."

"What is going on?" Michael demanded as he tried to make his way up onto his feet while making sure his boxer shorts weren't gaping open.

The woman nodded at him. "I feel like asking that question all the time."

She held her camera in one hand and brought up a piece of paper she had pulled out of one of her pockets with the other.

" 'Goodwives,' " she said as she scanned the paper. " 'These people had little, they wasted little, and the Earth suffered little while under their care.' Wow. That's deep."

She handed the paper to Michael. "Now that you know I'm here, I'll take some staged shots. Why don't you read this over so we can try to capture the mood Nora wants."

Michael looked down at the sheet, which had come out of someone's printer.

Draft 1: The Earth's Wife in the 21st Century
~~Diverting Solid Waste~~
~~Conserving Resources By Diverting Waste~~
~~Good Wives Don't Waste~~
~~Recalling the Goodwives of Other Centuries~~
Goodwives
~~Those of us, male and female, whose greatest goal~~
~~in life is to be good wives to the Earth, always bear~~
~~in mind that our . . . any . . . every wife has a great~~
~~responsibility for conserving her family's resources~~.

Every wife bears a major responsibility for conserving her family's resources. The Earth's Wife is no different. Casting aside usable materials that were made from the Earth's limited resources is as foolhardy as making frivolous expenditures with our family's limited resources. This is a constant in the lives of ~~wives~~ good wives.

Think back a few hundred years to the days when good wives were referred to as "goodwives." (NOTE: 17th century? Check.) Our Goodwife ancestors knew the word conserve. They didn't know the word disposable. Every material item they owned was used for decades, sometimes generations. These people had little, they wasted little, and the Earth suffered little while under their care.

Now, in the twenty-first century, it is time for a return to the concept of the Goodwife, a Goodwife being one who doesn't waste. On page   you'll find an

article on "trash" and the attractive and useful items
that it can be turned into.

There was more—much more—far more than Michael
wanted to read first thing in the morning. Or perhaps ever.

"Why didn't she just delete the stuff she decided not to
use?" he asked. "It's so much more work to put a line through
text like that."

"Nora likes to preserve the creative experience. Don't ask me
what that means. A better question would be why did she use
that first sentence? Don't you think it's sort of sexist?" the photographer said as she moved around the room and Michael
read. "I bet she'll change it. She'll say something about how
'wife' is a concept that has nothing to do with gender and anyone can be one."

Michael tried again to make sense of the paper he was holding while keeping his crotch covered. He finally gave up, on the
paper at least, and asked where Nora was.

"Around. She has some sort of morning routine. Fortunately, I don't, or having her call me at five A.M. the way she did
today would really, really bother me—sort of the way it bothered my husband when the phone rang an hour and a half before he had to get up."

Michael tried to cover himself with a pillow.

"I sure hope you're the Roberta who Nora said was going to
take pictures here today," he said anxiously.

"If I'm not, this is really disturbing, isn't it? Would you do me a favor and move that bag over there a little closer to the bed?"

This is really disturbing even if you are Roberta, Michael thought as he leaned over and pulled a bag toward him. He overdid it and tipped its contents onto the bed.

"Oh, gross. Old panty hose! Why would anyone keep old panty hose?" Michael exclaimed. "Unless you were some kind of sick guy, of course. In movies guys who collect panty hose are always really, really twisted."

"I used to use old panty hose for stuffing when I made puppets for my kids or throw pillows. I wonder if Nora and Walt would mind if I take some of them."

"I bet they'd let you have all of them."

Michael quickly started to pack the stockings back into their bag.

"Oh, no, don't do that! Not yet! Those panty hose dripping over the side of the bed like that makes everything just a little racy and off-color. I like it."

Michael looked around. "I get it. It makes it look as if I had a really wild night here."

"Yeah. This is going to look great. Now, could you get back up on the bed and look sort of bored and worn out, as if you have way too many things but they don't make you happy and you're tired of it all?"

"Unhappy? Tired of it all? Sure, I can do that. Give me a minute to comb my hair."

"No! Don't touch your hair! It looks surprised, just the way I want it."

Roberta's camera snapped away, and Michael thought, I'm almost positive this is going to be one of those things I'm going to live to regret.

"It's Nora's morning to make breakfast," Roberta Ferguson, art director for *The Earth's Wife,* explained to Michael after they had finished with their pictures and he had showered and dressed in black Dockers and a black dress shirt with a matching black tie. He hoped he looked as if he wanted to make a good impression, but not very badly. That way, if he was expected to dress up on his first day at the office, well, there was the tie hanging from his neck. But if he wasn't expected to dress up, the all-black outfit would make him appear as if he didn't care about making an impression in any traditional sense.

At least that was his plan.

"Nora makes two breakfasts," Roberta continued while they were standing in the kitchen at one end of the house's main room. "A cold bran cereal with soy milk during warm weather and a hot bran cereal with maple syrup during cold. She told us to pretend it's January because the cold cereal went stale while they were away and they're out of soy milk."

"If it's Nora's morning to make breakfast, how come you're doing it?" Michael asked Roberta.

"I always make it when I'm invited for breakfast on Nora's day. She's too slow. She can't do anything until she's finished that morning routine of hers. Besides, I know where they keep the raisins and the almonds, which makes hot bran cereal a whole lot easier to choke down. Nora actually likes the taste of plain bran cereal. Walt doesn't, but he won't say so because he thinks it isn't 'manly.' How long are you staying with them?"

"I don't know. We never talked about it."

Roberta handed him a bowl. "They really aren't into things like time."

The kitchen shared a wall with the downstairs bathroom. From the other side they heard a toilet flush. The shower started running, and then the door to the shower stall shut. Almost instantly a long stream of obscenities poured out of the bathroom, and then Walt shouted, "What happened to all the hot water?"

"You know, I was wondering about that, too. It was getting really cold in my shower by the time I was finished," Michael said.

Roberta laughed. "You were up there for quite a while. You must have used all the hot water."

"Oops."

They both looked toward the bathroom door. Walt was stamping and slamming things on the other side.

"He seems to have a bad temper," Michael said.

"Walt? Oh, no. He's a lovely man. Everyone loves Walt."

"SHIT!!"

"That's what I keep hearing," Michael agreed, sounding as if he were not entirely convinced. "My father says he loved Walt when he was a kid because Walt was the first grown-up who let him call him by his first name."

"Me, too!" Roberta exclaimed. "I grew up here and went to

a cooperative nursery school with Walt's kids. All the parents had to take turns helping out, and whenever Walt was at the school, he let us all call him Walt."

"My grandmother ran that school! Do you remember her?" Michael asked.

Roberta thought for a minute. "I remember her husband. Whenever it was his turn to help out at the school, he would make us all wash our hands before snacks and take naps."

"Oh, yeah, that's Poppy. He did that kind of thing with us, too," Michael said.

"But Walt, he would come to the school with a guitar and sing 'We Shall Overcome' with us. On baking days he never cared how big a mess we made. And once he took us on a field trip to march with some picketers who were on strike at a cheese factory. We were probably the only four-year-olds there."

They heard the shower stall door being slammed shut again and some loud muttering coming closer toward the door into the kitchen. Michael pushed himself away from the kitchen counter he had been leaning against while he ate. "I'm finished."

"You did remember to turn off the lights upstairs, didn't you?" Roberta asked as he took off toward the stairs all the way at the other end of the room. "Walt's lovely and everything, but leaving lights on really sets him off."

From the sounds coming from behind him, Michael didn't believe he'd be able to get up the stairs, along the balcony, and into his own bedroom, let alone into the bathroom (where he was sure both the overhead and the vanity lights were on), before Walt got out into the kitchen. Though Michael would have enjoyed seeing Walt set off, he decided that, it being his first day of work and Walt being his boss, it really would be better if he, himself, was not the one to do it. So he ducked into the study, the room just past Walt and Nora's bedroom and just before the stairs, to avoid attracting Walt's attention.

I can check my e-mail! he thought as he veered toward the door. Do I have enough time to send some e-mail? he wondered as he rushed into the study. Can I . . .

His mind went blank for a moment. When it started working again, he realized he was staring at Nora. What is she doing? his brain roared inside his head. Oh! Oh, no! She *does* wear a bra. A black one. With matching panties.

"I'm so sorry," he gasped.

"Why?" Nora asked, without pausing in her work. "What happened?"

She stood with free weights in each hand in front of the book-lined walls and next to the counter full of computer equipment. As Michael stared, she shifted her weight from one hip to the other, back and forth, while she did a long series of overhead presses.

Spandex, Michael thought, relieved. Spandex . . . athletic girlie stuff. Okay, I can deal with that.

"I . . . I . . . used up all the hot water," he stammered.

Nora laughed as she leaned forward and began raising the weights up sideways and then bringing them together down by her knees. "I only need a little water in the mornings. I shower on afternoons when the solar collectors have been exposed to a lot of sun all day. It feels so good to be part of the ebb and flow of the earth's rhythm."

"Yeah. Ebb and flow," Michael babbled.

As Nora brought the weights together in front of her—over and over and over again—her upper arms pressed against her breasts, forming cleavage that was exposed over the top of her sports bra.

Spandex girlie things on an old lady, Michael thought. Oh, jeez.

He supposed that for a woman of her advanced years Nora looked pretty good in her skimpy workout wear. Her upper arms, Michael couldn't help noticing, were in much better shape than his own, and there was nothing hanging over the top of the little panty/shorts/whatever she was wearing. That was as much as he could take in before his vision began to blur.

I'm being struck blind, he thought hysterically. Thank God.

". . . and lifting weights maintains bone density," Nora concluded as she switched to bicep curls. "If you can maintain bone density, you can eliminate a lot of health problems that require prescription drugs. If you can stay off prescription drugs, you can avoid supporting the pharmaceutical industry, which is making a *fortune* off our medications. We did an article on that in *The Earth's Wife,* oh, just last year. Honestly, who *really* wants to support the pharmaceutical industry?"

Michael—who was quite certain that if he made it into some third-tier college, his mother's investments in pharmaceutical stock would be paying his tuition—smiled and nodded without committing himself to anything.

Nora sighed happily and placed her weights on a shelf. "Now, why don't I run out to the kitchen and make you some breakfast?"

Because you're almost naked for starters, Michael thought.

"Ms. Ferguson made breakfast," he told her, his dry mouth barely able to form the words.

"I should have known. She likes to make breakfast so she can sneak raisins and almonds into the cereal. Well, then, I'll go get dressed, and once I've written in my journal, we'll be ready to head off to the office. Do you keep a journal, Michael? No? Try it. I guarantee that fifteen minutes of freewriting in a journal every morning will fire up your creativity for hours."

There's something I've always wanted to do, Michael thought.

Still, Nora was so enthusiastic about all her interests, it was easy to be swept along with them. So after she had left the room—and he had control of his limbs again—he picked up a five-pound weight off the shelf and began absentmindedly lifting it up and down. He stayed in the study, huddled against the door, unable to think of anything other than that he had to make sure nothing like this ever happened to him again.

The sound of a car starting finally cleared his head, and he recalled that he would never have been in the study in the first place if he hadn't been trying to avoid Walt. He listened carefully, but everything was silent. Where was Walt? In his bedroom? In the kitchen?

Waiting for me in *my* room? Michael asked himself.

He finally opened the door a crack. When that felt safe, he opened it a little farther. And then a little farther. There was no one in that portion of the house.

It was only a few steps to the stairs. Michael took them in as casual a manner as possible, just in case someone popped out from somewhere and saw him. Then he zipped up the stairs and along the balcony.

Walt didn't seem to be anywhere. Michael had forgotten about the bathroom lights by that time and left them on while he went to work packing Styrofoam beans into plastic bags, of which he had so many. He tied the bags shut with old panty hose and tossed them over the balcony to the living room below, planning to take them into the office of *The Earth's Wife* along with the bubble packing Nora had offered to send there the night before. Then he bagged up the rest of the panty hose and set it aside for Roberta.

The room, he had to admit when he'd finished, looked almost untouched—in large part, perhaps, because he hadn't made the bed. Still, he knew he was going to sleep better with what he thought was easily a trunk load of trash somewhere else.

"What's all this?" Nora asked when she came out of the house, fully dressed, and found him piling bags next to the car.

"Gar . . . Packing material to take to the office," Michael explained.

"Oh, we should have sent that in with Roberta. Walt

hitched a ride with her, so it's just the two of us. Hmmm. Well, we can take some of it."

"We can get it all in," Michael called confidently after Nora as she walked around the back of the house.

He followed her to a shed at the end of a large garden. She signaled for him to come closer as she opened the door. Before he could actually get in through the opening, she was pushing a couple of worn backpacks with metal frames at him. Even before the bicycles followed the backpacks, he'd started to develop a bad feeling about the situation.

"We'll get what we can into the backpacks, and you can use Walt's bike. We have a guest bike, but Walt's has baskets on either side of the back wheel, so you can carry more."

"Is there something wrong with the car?" Michael asked.

"Not that I know of."

"You don't drive! I forgot. That's all right. I can drive us."

"Oh, we never drive to work," Nora said. "That's why we built the house here instead of up in the mountains near the commune. We had to use the car every day when we lived there. Farmers can be self-sufficient living far from a town, but anyone who works in an office each day really needs to be close to a municipal center in order to minimize fossil-fuel consumption."

"That sounds like something you must have done an article on in . . . what? Ninety-seven? Ninety-eight?" Michael said miserably as he thought of Walt riding to work in luxury next to Roberta.

"Ninety-five, I think. It was about community planning."

I bet Roberta uses the air conditioner in her car, Michael told himself as he pushed the bike, an old three-speed with a wire basket over the handlebars and a fender over the back wheel from which two more baskets hung, back toward the Volvo. He dropped the backpack onto the ground and started loading it.

Anybody who sees me lugging all this stuff on a bike is going to think I'm homeless, he thought angrily as he forced a bag of beans into the backpack. Not that I'm unsympathetic to the plight of the homeless or anything. I just don't want to be mistaken for one. And just how am I supposed to balance and steer this old wreck with all this crap hanging off it and me? I'm going to lose control and end up in front of a truck or something. Won't that be sweet? And what about a helmet? Do these people think granola and clean air will fix a traumatic brain-stem injury? Only a . . .

"Catch!" Nora called merrily. Michael looked up in time to see a battered and scratched plastic bicycle helmet sailing toward him. Three of what looked like Walt's long, gray hairs were caught in the strap.

"So, how far away is the office?" Michael asked as he straddled the bicycle seat and finished strapping on the helmet, his baskets loaded, his pack strapped uncomfortably to his back.

"A mile if we go the short way. Now, if—"

"We better get going then," Michael broke in. He pushed off before Nora could suggest they take the long route.

Nora pulled ahead of him on the street so they could ride single file. Michael concentrated on not veering unexpectedly in front of traffic and wondered what he would be doing once they reached the office.

Was it too much to hope that he would be some kind of intern like Jonathan? Those kinds of things generally just didn't happen to him. Michael shot a glance over his shoulder at Nora, who was peddling along without much effort behind him. His grandfather had made that crack about her being rich and famous. The rich part was hard to believe, though Michael supposed she might have saved quite a bit of cash over the years by not using her car much or buying red meat. It would be terrific if Walt and Nora did have a lot of money, because Michael had read that office interns sometimes made as much as six hundred dollars a week. They sometimes got things like relocation expenses, insurance, maybe even a clothing allowance. There were more than five weeks left in the summer. If he worked for *The Earth's Wife* for five weeks, he wondered if he would be able to afford his own apartment. He didn't know anyone at school who had had their own apartment for five weeks. Or at all, for that matter.

Michael was beginning to feel hopeful—an emotion he didn't have a lot of experience with. He was also worrying about the state of his hair under the bicycle helmet and trying to keep the lower bar of the backpack frame from rubbing his back raw. Then they turned off the residential street Nora lived on and headed into the more developed business area of East Branbury. At eight-thirty in the morning the street was only occupied by others arriving for work at the shops, stopping at the bakery, or passing through on their way somewhere else.

Still, there was more traffic than they'd encountered so far, and Michael thought there was a very good chance he wouldn't be able to safely negotiate his way among the cars.

His anxiety was aggravated when Nora suddenly threw her left arm out in a hand signal Michael hadn't bothered learning when he was studying for his driver's test. She whipped across the lane of oncoming traffic, shot down an alley, and disappeared. Michael was afraid to brake too suddenly—he was sure the weight of the backpack he was carrying would send him over the handlebars and onto the street. He was at the end of the block before he was able to come to a stop. He decided to get off and push back to the spot where he'd last seen Nora, which made him feel like a wuss, but at least there was no one he knew in town who could see him.

The alley she'd headed into pitched downhill, and Michael was glad he wasn't riding any longer. It was all he could do to hold the bike back as he walked along beside it. At the bottom of the hill he heard Nora calling him. She was leaning against a bike rack, her helmet off, her backpack held in front of her like a bag of groceries.

"I'm sorry." She laughed. "I was thinking and forgot you were behind me. You did a good job finding your way here."

"Here" was a small parking lot behind one of the buildings that lined the main street. From a distance, the building had looked quaint and picturesque. Up close it looked old and maybe not entirely safe.

They're not going to be able to pay an intern six hundred

dollars a week, Michael told himself. I'll be lucky if I don't have to pay them.

The offices of *The Earth's Wife* were on the second floor. To reach them, they had to climb a metal stairway past the back of a street-level store that was being renovated. They could hear a saw whining inside the shop on the ground floor as well as something that sounded like lumber being dropped.

"We're having this work done so we'll finally have space for Earth's Publications," Nora said, stopping long enough for them to poke their heads in the door and see that the space was being partitioned into a number of smaller rooms. "And we need offices for a children's environmental magazine we're going to try next year—*The Earth's Child.* Don't you love the title?"

"It sounds like something my grandmother would have bought me for Christmas when I was little."

Nora stopped on the stairs and turned around to look at him. "Do you think so? I've wanted to do it for ages, but I didn't have time until we got a managing editor for *The Earth's Wife,*" she confided, her voice full of excitement. "Our reader-ship is *desperate* for a magazine like ours for their children. We should have started it years ago."

Oh, thank God you didn't, Michael thought as Nora opened a door with a picture of the Earth, looking intensely green and blue, painted on it.

The sound of construction was muffled as soon as they closed the door, and Michael was relieved to see that the first room they entered looked as if normal people might work in it. It took up one end of the building and was white and gray with framed *Earth's Wife* covers artfully arranged on the walls. There were filing cabinets and computer equipment behind a counter that divided the room into reception and work areas. A nice couch and some easy chairs were arranged in one corner.

"Amber!" Nora exclaimed happily. "What are you doing here?"

A seventeen- or eighteen-year-old girl looked up from where she was sorting mail. "Don't worry. Hell didn't freeze over while you were away. I'm just filling in for Annette. She's in court with one of those lowlife sons of hers, so I graciously agreed to answer the phones and sign for packages," Amber said, popping up from behind her desk. Below her modest twin sweater set she was wearing what Michael found to be a distractingly short red skirt.

A short red skirt that she is really a little too large to be wearing, Michael noticed.

Nora shook her head and smiled. "Was Todd surprised?"

"That one of Annette's kids is in court? I don't see how he could have been. It's got to be the third or fourth time with Kyle, and they say he's nothing compared with his older brother. There is an established pattern of behavior here that even Todd ought to recognize."

Amber wore a look of extreme—and very fake—innocence.

"I meant, was Todd surprised that *you* were the person Annette found to fill in for her?" A look of suspicion suddenly streaked across Nora's face. "Annette did tell him that you were going to cover for her, didn't she?"

"Todd asked me to come in himself."

"No!"

"Yes! Well, where else was he going to find someone to come in for just one day? He was damn lucky it was my day off or he'd be answering his own phone and signing for his own packages. You know how he hates to do things like that . . . or helping to clean up after lunch meetings . . . or being the one who goes out to buy toilet paper . . ."

Nora pulled a pair of glasses out of her backpack and used them to read the mail. "Take my advice and don't mention buying toilet paper in front of Todd," she said absently. "There was an awful scene between him and Walt when he came back with those padded rolls that had no post-consumer recycled content."

Amber sighed. "I wish I could have been here for that."

"Who's Todd?" Michael asked.

"Our managing editor," Nora said. "Amber, this is Michael. Michael, this is Amber, who is filling in for Annette today. Michael's grandparents were friends of ours in days of old," Nora explained to Amber. "He's going to spend some time with us this summer and give us a hand around here."

"Uh-oh. Todd won't be happy about that. But maybe I can help you out," Amber offered, looking at Michael. "I'm planning to conduct aversion therapy with him today. You know how if people are afraid of snakes and they're forced to handle them, they get over their fear? At least theoretically? Well, if Todd is forced to have me here, he might get over his fear of people under twenty-five, people who don't have college degrees, and people who don't kiss his ass. All at once! Except— am I talking about therapy or am I talking about a miracle?"

Michael could feel sweat marks forming where his shirt covered his armpits. Great, he thought. Now I've got to remember to keep my arms down all day.

"What exactly do you have in mind for me to do here?" Michael asked in a low voice as Nora led him down a long, dark hallway lined with opened doors.

"Oh, Todd will have plenty for you to do," Nora assured him.

At the end of the hallway was a door that led into a room that took up the width of the building, just as the reception area had at the other end of the hall. This room, though, was short, making up in breadth what it lacked in length. They entered it and Nora confided, "Todd came here from a magazine with a bigger staff than ours. It's been a year and a half, and he's still having trouble getting used to the fact that we don't have lots of people to do all the little things."

Walt was sitting at one of the cluttered tables that lined the room and peering through his glasses at a spreadsheet. "Oh, yeah," he said. "He still misses all his little slavies."

"But will this Todd want me working here?" Michael asked anxiously. "I'm under twenty-five, and I haven't been to college, you know. Don't you? And my ass-kissing skills . . . well . . ."

"They could use a little work," Walt agreed.

"Are you worried about what Amber just said?" Nora asked. "Don't give it a thought. Todd doesn't hate young people. Amber thinks he does because he . . . well . . . he does have a . . . little objection . . . to *her*. She doesn't know, which is why she *thinks* he hates everyone her age. And no one has set her straight because it would be so unkind to tell her that someone . . . dislikes . . . her not because she's young but because she's . . . Amber."

"Oh, Nora, you're being way too sensitive," Walt objected. "Todd hates me, and I don't care. Amber wouldn't, either."

"Michael, I promise you, Todd doesn't hate anybody. He just has had a little trouble getting along with Amber and Walt," Nora said.

"Oh, I'm sure we're not the only ones."

"Walt, you're making Michael anxious," Nora chided.

"No, really, I'm fine," Michael lied.

"Don't worry, kid," Walt said. "Todd's going to love you. Actually, he's probably going to like me better, too, after I give you to him. He's just the type to want an office peon."

"Pee on?" asked Michael.

Nora had sat down at another table and was moving a stack of magazines to one side. "Someone who's been forced into servitude to work off some sort of debt," she said as she looked at a cover.

It won't be easy to make that sound good in an e-mail to Jonathan, Michael thought despondently. But all he said was, "And how does that pay?"

FIVE

The office peon position was not going to pay well enough for Michael to get his own place; a campsite, maybe, assuming he could borrow a tent, but not an apartment. He wasn't actually surprised. People *did* go from hourly jobs watering lawns for relatives to salaried office positions that provided dream incomes. They were just always *other* people.

By quarter after nine he was sitting in front of a computer in a spare office. He had already been awakened by a strange woman in his bedroom, had to escape from his enraged host, walked in on an embarrassing scene involving his hostess, learned that he was going to be riding an old bike to work every day, and been told that his paychecks for the next few weeks weren't going to break the bank they were drawn upon. He felt as if he'd been working all day.

He stared at the monitor in front of him and read the letter that appeared on it.

To the Editor:

I very much enjoyed last month's article on the pollution caused by vehicles using drive-up windows at fast-food restaurants and banks. You only have to sit in a line of cars waiting ten minutes or more for a couple of burgers and a shake, as I have done many times, to realize our atmosphere is being poisoned. Last week I used drive-up windows at a bank twice and a drugstore once. Isn't it awful that you can get your prescriptions at drive-up windows now? It ought to be a crime, all those cars sitting there with their engines running. I counted eight the last time I was at Burger King. I wouldn't have used the drive-up that day, myself, but it looked as if there was no place to sit inside anyway.

He looked at his watch and wondered when it would be time to leave for the day.

He was sorting e-mails to the editor and placing them in storage files. Later in the day he would be instructed on how to respond to them because *"The Earth's Wife* and her readers are a community."* That was what Nora had told him when she gave him the e-mail reading task while they were waiting for Todd to return from a talk he was giving at a breakfast conference at the University of Vermont. "We communicate with one another just like members of a community."

To the Editor:

Why doesn't *The Earth's Wife* do an article on the extraterrestrials who are infiltrating our educational system as well as our military and government? You do stories on subjects no one else will touch. So why not this one? Aliens are only interested in plundering our natural resources. What do you think that would do to our ecosystem?

This may not be a community I want to belong to, Michael thought as he filed that message in "Complaints."

The task left a large portion of his mind free. He was able to use it to wonder about Todd Mylnarski. Is it really all that bad a thing that Todd doesn't like Walt? he wondered. I'm not exactly crazy about him myself. My grandfather doesn't seem to care for him all that much, either. Oh, no. What if Todd and Poppy are alike?

"Yeah, we had a great time," he heard Walt saying to someone out in the hall. "The family couldn't be better. We've finally lived long enough to see our grandkids become teenagers and make our sons' lives miserable the way they made our lives miserable through a big chunk of the seventies. I can die a happy man."

Walt's voice had been coming closer. The next time he spoke, he was standing right outside the door to Michael's office.

"I brought you something," he said.

Another man's voice said, "A kid? You brought me a kid? What will I do with him?"

"Anything you want. I'm paying him. All you have to do is find something for him to do."

Michael's desk and chair were positioned in a right angle to the door, so he only had to look to one side to see the men in the doorway talking about him. The new man stepped forward with his arm extended.

"Todd Mylnarski," he said.

"Michael Racine," Michael replied as they shook hands. He didn't think to stand up until after they were grasping one another, which meant he had to struggle out of his chair while holding hands with another guy.

Not good, he had to admit.

Todd was younger than Michael had expected, which was not to say he was actually young—he was just younger than Michael's parents and considerably younger than Walt. He had some wrinkles, but he wasn't gray or bald, and his pants weren't too snug the way so many older guys' pants were. He was tall and thin and okay-looking in a very run-of-the-mill sort of way. He was also dressed in a gray dress shirt and black tie.

Hey, gray is a lighter shade of black! Michael realized. I'm dressed right!

"So, Michael, you're interested in working for a magazine," Todd said. It wasn't a question, which was good because it meant there was nothing Michael felt he had to say in response. But it wasn't exactly accurate, either, because he wasn't actually interested in working for *a* magazine. He was just interested in working for *this* one, and only because it would keep him away from home for a while.

"Have you worked on a school magazine or newspaper?" Todd asked.

"No, actually—"

"How are your English grades?"

"Oh, well—"

"I get it," Todd said, frowning and nodding his head. "You're here because you're an environmentalist, right?"

Walt started to laugh.

"Michael has communication skills," Nora explained as she joined them. "We thought he could be very useful here for a few weeks. While he was waiting for you to get back from your conference, he started sorting all those e-mails that need to be responded to."

Todd's eyebrows shot up. "That *is* a good idea," he said as he stepped back out into the hall, drawing Walt and Nora with him.

He came back by himself before Michael could get settled and back to work.

"Listen, Mike, while you're sorting those e-mails, I'd like you to do something else for me," he said, drawing up a chair and sitting down next to Michael. "Keep track of which articles *The Wife* readers mention most frequently and whether they are responding positively or negatively to them. Just pull some paper out of the printer over there and make a rough chart of some kind. Nothing fancy. We need to know what readers want to see in the magazine. Understand?"

Michael nodded. "Sure. It's like having a counter on a Web site. Or television ratings. Except you're doing it for magazine articles."

"Right! And listen . . ." Todd lowered his voice. "If you find letters from the obviously insane, forward them to me. I love that stuff."

"You'll probably get a lot. I haven't noticed all that many messages from people who are obviously *sane,*" Michael said.

Todd laughed appreciatively. "I just wish I had time to go through the mail myself. It's great stuff."

"Yeah, I guess it is," Michael realized.

Todd suddenly became very serious. "You have to laugh at some of these people because if you didn't, you'd have to cry for them." He paused, as if in prayer. Then he clapped Michael on the back and said, "Glad to have you here."

I was right—Todd's not getting along with Walt is a good thing, Michael thought as he forwarded him the extraterrestrial message he'd read earlier and went on with his work.

Dear *Earth's Wife,*

Kudos on another wonderful issue!

One suggestion—Have you ever considered doing a fiction issue? No one is publishing eco-fiction right now. I don't know why. You could do a special issue once a year on ecologically themed literature the way *Sports Illustrated* does a special issue once a year on women's swimsuits. Look how much people look forward to that!

And as for Todd not getting along with Amber?

Amber. Okay, her hair is kind of limp, and it's hard to tell whether it's dark blond or light brown. And she's kind of tall . . . and I guess what they call big-boned . . . and scary-looking. But she's a girl. And only a year or two older than I am, which is close enough and, actually, a good thing because older women are supposed to know stuff. Everybody says so—though no one actually says what it is they're supposed to know, Michael realized.

There were a few things, at least, that he was sure Amber *didn't* know. She didn't know that he hadn't had a girlfriend since third grade, for example. She didn't know he hadn't gone to the Freshman Reception. She didn't know that he'd never been out alone with a girl in his entire life and that when he went out with groups, for some reason girls always managed to sit one seat away from him. She didn't know that at the rate he was going, his younger brother might start dating before he did.

In all the excitement of the last forty-eight hours, it had never occurred to Michael to even consider the possibility of whether or not he'd be running into any age-appropriate women. Now that it did occur to him, he had lots to consider.

Maybe, he thought, I'll hate living with Walt and Nora, and I won't make a whole lot of money, and the job won't be great, *but* I'll have a summer romance! And if I do, I want it to be a really hot one.

He kept looking at his watch and wondering how he could find an excuse to go back out into the reception area. At quarter after eleven he thought of one.

The room he was using was next to Nora's office at the far end of the hall, meaning Michael would have to walk past Roberta's open door and the library, to his right, and two more small offices to his left.

"Mr. Mylnarski is on another line," Amber was saying when

Michael finally reached the reception area. "May I take a message?"

Michael picked up a copy of the most recent issue of *The Wife* from the stack on the table next to the couch and patiently stared at the cover, casually moving back and forth from one foot to the other.

"Douglas Sinclair . . . okay. No, I'm sorry, he didn't give me any messages for you. . . . Oh. Oh. Wait. Who's threatening you? . . . Mr. Mylnarski?"

Michael turned to look at Amber. She was rolling her eyes and struggling to keep from laughing.

"I'm sorry. I'll definitely give him your message and tell him you're waiting to hear from him. . . . No, really, I'll do it myself. . . . I'll hand it to him. I won't even leave it on his desk. . . . I promise. . . . I'll do it. *Yes.* I'll do it."

Amber stood up as she hung up the phone. "This is going to be fun. You want to watch while I give Todd this message? It's a particularly psycho one."

"Actually, I need to go to the bathroom."

That didn't come out the way he thought it would.

"And?"

"Is there a bathroom here?"

Amber silently pointed to a closed door behind him.

Michael gave her a shot of his great smile (it was his best feature and he had his father and grandfather to thank for it), which she missed because she was already on her way to Todd's office. He stood there for a moment, grinning at nothing, then jumped when he heard the door behind him suddenly open. In order to get out of sight as soon as possible, he went charging through it, brushing past a strange woman on her way out. They passed so closely that she was pushed up against the door frame, and he worried that she would think he had felt her breasts through her thin, sleeveless sweater.

Which he did, but it was an accident, and, besides, he thought, maybe she didn't notice. She might not have noticed. Could she have noticed?

"Are you okay?" the woman called through the closed door.

"Fine! Just fine!"

What am I going to say to Amber? Michael kept wondering as he paced back and forth in the tiny bathroom. He tipped over a pile of pamphlets called *Water Quality Studies* that was stacked within reach of the commode. While bending down to tidy it up, he knocked a brown lump of avocado-and-goat's-milk soap off from the side of the sink into the trash.

I have to say something to get a conversation started, he told himself as he hurried to repair the damage he'd done on his first trip to the company bathroom. What? What can I say?

I could make some witty comments about world affairs. That always makes a guy look smart and sophisticated. Except I don't know about any world affairs, so the witty-comment thing doesn't seem very likely. Unless I made one accidentally. I suppose it could happen, but . . .

Music. Come on, Michael! You own more than a hundred CDs! You've memorized all the tour dates for Ozzfest. You can definitely say something about music.

Oh, right, moron. You're going to go up to a coworker and at eleven-fifteen in the morning start rambling on about Ozzy Osbourne. The time and place have to be just right for a discussion of heavy metal. Otherwise, you could end up sounding . . . sounding like someone who has nothing else to do but memorize the tour dates for Ozzfest.

He looked at himself in the mirror. If I stay in here much longer, she'll think I have some kind of condition and it won't matter what I say to her. Nobody wants to go out with a person who has some kind of condition that requires long stays in the bathroom. I know I don't.

He saw his eyebrows rise up on his forehead as an idea came to him.

I'll just nod casually as I walk by her desk, he told himself. I'll be mysterious. And if we never speak again, I will have the comfort of knowing that I was cool. And that she knew I was cool. And that I knew that she knew that I was cool.

Yeah.

He finally left the bathroom and headed toward Amber, who was back at her desk. He got closer and closer, waiting for her to lift her head so he could give her the sober, "I'm deep. I'm thinking serious thoughts. Don't you wish you knew me?" nod he'd been practicing in the bathroom. Maybe I should smile just a little bit, just on one side of my mouth, he thought. So I'll look mysterious but friendly.

"So, Michael, where do you stand on the issue of composting toilets?" Amber asked.

Michael stopped dead in his tracks and stared at her for a moment. Then he said, "What are my choices?"

"Composting toilets—those things with a container of some sort under the seat so when you flush, nothing goes very far? Then you throw a handful of bark mulch or some leaves in there with the crap, and it all decomposes?"

Michael started to grin. Okay! he thought ecstatically. *She's coming on to me.*

"What? You think I'm joking?" Amber asked, mistaking the look of joy on Michael's face for appreciation of toilet humor.

"Well, it doesn't sound much like a joke," Michael admitted, "not a very funny one, anyway. But it is kind of . . . an odd thought."

"You've never heard of composting toilets, have you? Well, you're lucky I brought it up, because you're going to. It's, like, a big political issue here," Amber explained. She took a deep breath as if getting ready for a long speech. Her sweater rose up as her lungs—and her chest—expanded. "At one end of the spectrum you've got your people who want to see all human waste transformed into nutrients in a box under their johns and used to fertilize public parks and gardens so they can feel a sense of unity with their environment. At the other end you've got folks who don't understand why the federal government isn't committing big bucks to researching ways to vaporize their doodie like they do on *Star Trek* so they'll never have to think about it again."

"They vaporize doodie on *Star Trek*?" Michael asked.

Amber looked up at him. "Haven't you always been curious?"

"I don't actually watch *Star Trek* much. It's my little brother's thing. He builds rockets, designs space stations in art class, watches *Star Trek*—"

"Cool kid. Well, if you're here very long, the subject of composting toilets is going to come up. You'd think we were talking stem-cell research the way they carry on about it. It's a very divisive issue."

"This *is* a joke, then," Michael said while thinking, Cool kid? Eddie?

"Try laughing when you hear someone talking about it. You'll see how funny it is. What have they got you doing here, anyway?"

"Reading e-mails that come in from readers."

"I did that last summer. The people who send e-mails to *The Wife* are so much crazier than the ones who use the postal service. It's as if knowing they haven't included their address makes them feel free to give full rein to their mental instability."

"You worked here last summer?" Michael asked. "What are you doing this year?"

"I'm a lifeguard at the town pool."

A lifeguard like Lindsey. Michael so wanted a chance with a lifeguard. Amber started to become beautiful right before his eyes.

"You're going to love working here," Amber told him. "It's like being in the midst of a pack of animals."

"And that's good?"

"It's incredible." Amber signaled for Michael to come closer. " 'This one' wants 'that one's' job. 'This one' wants 'that one' fired. 'This one' doesn't get along with 'that one,' and now, this year, 'this one' is 'involved' with 'that one.' I would name names, but gossiping is so unprofessional."

She seemed to think she was being quiet and confidential, but Michael was uncomfortably aware that they were in a room that anyone could come walking into at any moment.

"They only have four regular staff members here," Amber continued. "Todd, the managing editor, Nora, the publisher, Roberta, the art director, and Maureen, the associate editor. Five if you count Walt, who does whatever he wants and only when he wants to . . . six if you count the on-line editor, who doesn't like to come into the office much . . . well, seven, I guess, because he has at least one person doing geek jobs for him. Oh, and then there's Annette. Well, my point is, this is not a big place. But since Todd came, there's just *so* much going on, if you know what I mean."

"I guess."

"You see," Amber continued, warming up to her subject, "Todd is an alpha male—or he thinks he is. He wants to be the top guy in the group. Walt doesn't think he is an alpha male, but he is. He may have been doing his share of the housework for forty years or so and taking care of the grandkids when they came to visit and all that, but he was still always the top guy around here. Well, usually Nora makes a big point of hiring women because sisterhood is supposed to be powerful or something, so nobody really noticed Walt was an alpha male because he was generally the only male around. But once Todd showed up last summer, he and Walt started fighting to see which one of them would get to dominate all the other workers just like the biggest, strongest males fight for the dominant alpha, or top, position in a pack of animals."

My father is the only male in his office since Poppy retired, *and* he's the boss. He must be the alpha male, Michael reasoned. No, it's probably that bitchy office manager of his, Mrs. Franken. Poor Dad. He's the only man there, and he still can't be the alpha guy. Just watch, that's how I'm going to end up.

"You'll see what I'm talking about if you're here very long. The work here for students really sucks—answering the phones is about as good as it gets—so when there's students working here, Walt lets them sit in on all kinds of meetings so they can at least see how things work around here. He's very big on 'power to the people,' 'everybody's equal,' 'all work has value,' yada yada yada. Anyway, last spring I was able to do a paper on this place for my psychology class," Amber concluded as the woman Michael had felt up on his way into the bathroom came to a stop beside him.

"Michael? I'm Maureen Bogda," she announced.

"Associate editor," Amber reminded him. "Don't ask what that is. I was here all of July and August last year and never figured it out."

"We have something we'd like you to take care of for us. We need you to go out and pick up a few lunches," Maureen said as she handed Michael several orders with cash clipped to them and explained how he would find the restaurant.

Amber caught Michael's eye. "Speaking of sucky work—"

"Oh, no!" Michael objected. "I like buying things."

"I'm glad to hear that," Maureen said, "because Nora asked if you would stop at the little grocery store on the corner to pick up some soy milk and eggs. She wants the free-range eggs from chickens that have never lived in cages, if they have them this week. However, she says that if they are packed in a plastic package to please check and make sure the package is either number one or two plastic because that's all we can recycle in this town. If they have the free-range eggs, but they're packed in the wrong kind of plastic, don't get them. Get regular eggs, but make sure the regular eggs are in a cardboard package, not Styrofoam, because Nora doesn't buy Styrofoam."

"Uh . . . just a minute. I'd better write that down," Michael said as he started to look over Amber's desk, hoping to find some paper.

"Nora did it for you," Maureen replied as she handed Michael another piece of paper and some more money. Finally, she held out a ten-dollar bill. "And Walt says for you to pick up some lunch for yourself, too."

"Gee, thanks," Michael said as his instructor disappeared back down the hall.

"That's the difference between Walt and Todd," Amber concluded. "Walt is the kind of alpha male who buys lunch. Todd is the kind of alpha male who doesn't."

"You really seem to be into this place. Why aren't you working here this summer?" Michael asked.

Amber's face suddenly became hard and still. "Because I hate Todd," she hissed.

"Oh, well," Michael said awkwardly. "Ah . . . can I get you

some lunch?" he asked suddenly, waving Walt's ten-dollar bill at her. "I'll pay."

And if I pay, I'm calling it a date, he told himself. We will be on our way!

Amber perked up again. "Oh, no," she said cheerfully. "I'm making my mother take me out to lunch today."

I was so close, Michael thought sadly as he headed out the door.

Six

That afternoon, Michael found himself sitting at the round table in the office library while a staff meeting was being conducted around him. What he was supposed to be doing while he was sitting there wasn't very clear to him. He guessed it was part of Walt's power to the people/everybody's equal/all work has value/yada yada yada thing that Amber had told him about. Though, personally, he would much rather be doing his peon labor—reading crazy e-mails—than sitting there listening to an intense discussion on whether *The Earth's Wife* should support the environmental group that had been claiming the March equinox as Earth Day for over thirty years or give its backing to the environmental group that had been claiming April 22 as Earth Day for over thirty years. He didn't know anyone who cared about Earth Day whenever it occurred, so he spent his time trying to guess who wanted someone else's job, who wanted someone else fired, who didn't get along with someone else, and, most importantly, who was "involved" with someone else, who that someone else might be, and just what "involved" meant.

He looked around the table. Todd was sitting on one side with Maureen next to him. Nora was across from them with Walt next to her, though his chair was pushed away from the table so he was a little behind her with one leg crossed over the other. Michael and Roberta were also across from each other, about halfway between the other two pairs.

Okay, Michael began. Todd seems like a likely candidate for some of Amber's categories. I already know he doesn't get along with Walt and Amber, so that takes care of one right there. Of course, Michael realized, Walt and Amber were the ones who told him Todd didn't get along with them. Maybe *Todd* thought he got along with them just fine. In which case, did he fit into that category at all? How could a person decide if someone didn't get along with someone else? All right, Michael told himself, just forget about that for a while. Think about whether or not Todd might want to have someone fired. This managing-editor job of his seems to involve finding freelance writers, bugging everyone about how fast and how hard they're working, and meddling in everything. He probably can actually fire someone, and if he can, wouldn't he want to? What about dating another staff member? He does have that cool outfit on.

Michael hoped Maureen hadn't noticed that he'd groped her on his way into the bathroom that morning. He worried that she was giving him funny looks. From what he'd been able to figure out, her job seemed to involve writing titles, the table of contents, and some regular columns, as well as copyediting. Maybe she wants Todd's job as managing editor, he decided. If I had to do what she does for a living, I'd sure want someone else's job. She could also be seeing someone. Her hair's kind of an unnatural shade of black (could she have dyed it to match the frames of her glasses?), but she's still the hottest woman here just because she's the youngest. Plus, she has no obvious scars or moles or anything. She's almost a babe. Almost.

Unless Roberta was out for the managing editor's position, too, just for the sake of being able to boss people around, it was not very likely she would want anyone else's job, Michael reasoned. She decided how the magazine's pages would look, chose fonts, and worked with photographers, none of which involved as much writing as the others had to do. She also had the best office. It was nearly as large and cluttered as the library. She might not like someone here, and she might want to see someone fired, but Michael didn't think she was dating somebody because, well, she had that big backside and a husband, the one who was mad when Nora called them too early.

Walt, Michael concluded, was the real contender for being the person who didn't get along with someone, especially since he'd said himself that Todd hated him. And he could easily see Walt wanting to get someone fired, just because he was Walt. But whose job would he want? Michael wondered. According to Amber, he did only what he wanted to do when he wanted to do it. You just don't find jobs better than that. As far as being involved with someone was concerned, Walt has Nora.

Then there was Nora. Nora likes to be part of the ebb and

flow of the earth's rhythm, Michael recalled, and she doesn't get cable because she thinks the airwaves should be free. She's just not ever going to do something like want someone else's job or not get along with somebody. And as far as being involved with someone—she has Walt.

But Michael did think she might fire someone who, say, ate an endangered pig or something.

He'd forgotten about Annette . . . and the on-line editor . . . and the on-line editor's geek.

You know what I need? Michael decided as Nora asked for a vote on the Earth Day issue. I need to make a chart with each person's name in a little circle and then I can draw lines from person to person until I've worked out all the possibilities—like the things they put in magazines when they want to be able to show how all the people in the White House are connected to one another. Or the people on *Survivor.*

"So, who's for the March date?" Nora asked after making her motion. "Roberta, Walt, and me. That leaves Todd and Maureen for April, and March passes. What's next, Todd?"

"Roberta and I have been talking about how we need to make more of a visual impact with our covers," Todd said. "Now, in January we're running a big story on Senator Dimauro, right? The photographer Roberta found in his state did some really nice work."

"It ended up costing us even more than I thought it would," Roberta said apologetically.

Nora shrugged. "He's a national figure, and we want this spread to look good."

Senator Dimauro, Senator Dimauro . . . have I heard of him? Michael didn't think so. But maybe . . .

"Dimauro *is* a national figure," Todd agreed eagerly. "A possible presidential contender, right? Interest in him is high. People want to read about him."

Michael shook his head just the slightest bit. No, I don't have a clue who this guy is.

"Now, our standard cover," Todd said as he held up the most recent issue of *The Earth's Wife*, "involves starting the major story right on the front of the magazine. No image, no cover lines to tip readers off that we have other articles they can read.

The Earth's Wife

Vol. 33 Iss. 6

You'll Be the Next to Go
BY KARL DOOME

School of Economics
University of Southern North Dakota

"What this country needs is a good recession. A real economic downturn would do us a world of good. Or an energy shortage. We need to do without a few things for a while. Or an energy shortage AND a recession. Yes, that's the ticket.

"The good times have lasted too long. Affluence, wealth, prosperity (whatever you want to call it) is killing us. You haven't noticed? Take a look out your window. A by-product of wealth is waste—all the excess you purchased and didn't need, didn't want, didn't keep. The Earth has to absorb that. She's the one it's killing.

"When she's gone, you'll be the next to go. And you'll be going soon."

Continued inside

Right? Just text, assuming that readers walking by a newsstand will dive right into the story and be hooked."

Michael scanned the cover Todd was holding.

Whew, that's depressing, Michael thought.

"I agree, this makes us different," Todd said. "No magazine does it every single month the way we have since back in the days when you guys were selling *The Wife* out of the trunk of your car at Laundromats and grocery stores. But there's a reason for that. Most magazines today use an image on their covers. A picture. And they use a picture because they can communicate faster with a picture. Right? Am I right? That means they can communicate to more people—all the people who wouldn't stop in front of a newsstand to read all this text."

"Right! That's right!" Michael exclaimed unexpectedly. "Oops. I said that out loud, didn't I? Sorry. But, you know, he's right. I think."

"Yes, he is," Maureen agreed eagerly.

Todd beamed over at Michael.

"So," he said, "Roberta worked up a sample cover for the Dimauro issue that the two of us feel would bring it to the attention of far more people than the cover we usually run would."

Roberta held up a presentation board. Michael studied it critically. *The Earth's Wife*'s logo appeared at the top, just as it did on the other board, but instead of text underneath it, there was a picture of a gray-haired man in a gray suit standing in front of the sort of blue-and-gray sky scene the school photographer used each year.

That's almost as gloomy as what they had before, Michael decided. Maybe you have to like being depressed to want to read this magazine.

Maureen jumped up and pointed to some short lines of text sprinkled around the edges of the gray suit. "With this cover we can use all these cute little cover lines that give readers a hint about the other articles we're running."

"This is a modern, up-to-date look for the magazine, designed to attract readers," Todd said, indicating the cover with the photo. "The other one—"

"Todd, we don't start our major stories on the cover in order to attract readers," Nora explained. "We do it so we aren't wasting any space. Every inch of the magazine is used for content. It's a value, a principle. *The Earth's Wife* is all about values. We do not waste."

"That's all very nice, but what about attracting readers?" Todd asked.

Walt spoke up for the first time. "We're attracting readers," he said.

"But we could attract more, right? And maybe attract some who don't think there's an alien conspiracy to destroy the environment?" Todd suggested. He waved a hard copy of what looked like an e-mail.

Michael straightened up. Is that the message I forwarded to him? Oh my gosh! I've only been here a few hours and already an e-mail I found is being mentioned at a staff meeting. Maybe I *do* have communication skills.

"Ah, there's a whole bunch of guys in New Mexico who are always sending us extraterrestrial messages," Walt said. "They're harmless."

"Maybe if we had a different kind of cover, we'd draw a different type of reader. A normal type, for instance," Todd replied.

If I do know anything about communication, it must be on a really instinctual level, Michael thought, because, really, I thought communication had something to do with satellites, but how are satellites connected with people having communication *skills*?

Suddenly Michael realized that the room had gone quiet and everyone was watching him.

What did I miss? What could they want? They had asked him to get lunch, but that had been over for a while.

"Did someone want coffee?" he finally asked. "Do you want me to go out and get some?"

"We don't drink coffee here," Nora explained. "The workers on the coffee plantations are exploited, you know, and by drinking coffee we'd be contributing to the exploitation. We're doing an article on it in a couple of months."

"We wanted you to pretend you're an average guy—a normal guy—walking past a magazine rack. A normal guy who knows nothing about *The Earth's Wife*," Todd said.

"Uh, I can do that."

"So, you see these two magazines on the rack, right?" Todd said, waving the last issue and pointing to the presentation board Roberta was still holding up. "Which one are you more likely to stop and look at?"

"That's easy," Michael said, breathing a sigh of relief. "I wouldn't look at either one of them."

"So much for your normal market," Walt said to Todd.

"He's just a kid. Don't put him on the spot," Roberta objected.

"You're right. I shouldn't have asked you, Mike. Forget about it. We still need to do something about these covers . . ."

Wait! Wait! What happened? A minute ago Todd was using the e-mail *I* found for him, and now he's treating me as if I just cut one?

"Excuse me," he said, his face red. "I would never see either of those magazines because bookstores organize the magazines on the rack by *type* of magazine. When I was little, I used to buy boating magazines for my father for his birthday because he has a kayak. All the boating magazines were together in one place. If I didn't know that there were boating magazines, I would never have just stumbled upon them, because back then all I read was *Mad,* and the people at the store didn't put the boating magazines with the humor magazines. Now I only read computer magazines and music magazines, and they aren't displayed with environmental magazines. I don't even look at anything else." Michael felt his face getting hotter. He cleared his throat. "Well, I do look at *some* other things, of course. Once in a while. But just the pictures. And I'm sure those sorts of magazines aren't displayed anywhere near yours. . . . Not that I look at those other things often enough to really know. . . . But I don't think so. . . ."

"Don't sweat it, kid," Walt said reassuringly. "We've got freedom of the press in this country. Porn has a right to exist, and you've got a right to look at it."

"Well, not really, Walt. He's not eighteen," Nora reminded him.

"Oh, yeah. In that case, we'll give you a twenty-minute head start and then we're calling the Feds," Walt warned.

"Porn! Who said anything about porn?" Michael exclaimed. "I was talking about . . . you know . . . men's magazines. They have articles about cars and stereos and stuff."

"Except you don't read those articles. You said you look at the pictures," Maureen reminded him. "What are the pictures of?"

Oh, antiperspirant, don't fail me now, Michael pleaded as he wiped some sweat from his forehead with the back of his hand and worried about the state of his pit stains.

"Has anyone else noticed," Roberta broke in, "that men's magazines have pictures of half-naked women, but women's magazines don't have pictures of half-naked men? What's that about?"

"Am I right in believing that this is not on the agenda?" Todd asked while the others were laughing. "Therefore, could we *please* get back to my cover, which is the topic under discussion?"

"I was just . . . just trying to say that I only know about *The Earth's Wife* because my relatives get it. I've never seen it with any of the magazines I look at in stores. So I don't think it matters what's on the cover. If people don't know about it, they aren't going to look for it. And if it's about a subject they aren't interested in, they aren't going to accidentally find it."

Did that sound smart? Michael wondered anxiously as he finished speaking. I don't even care if it made sense so long as I didn't sound like an idiot.

No one responded to his statement, which gave him plenty of time to think about his situation.

Working in an office is too hard. I never know what I should be saying. Porn! Did I actually say I look at porno magazines? And I never know what I should be doing, either. Though I'm guessing I shouldn't be talking about porn. The others know what they're supposed to do. *They* know not to start a conversation about porn. I have to be told every single thing. Why didn't somebody tell me not to talk about porn? I feel like a moron. I don't like this. Is there some way I can go home? Tonight? Even seeing Eddie off to science camp tomorrow morning would be better than this.

Some movement across the table finally caught Michael's attention. Todd was nodding his head as he pulled together his thoughts.

"I think what Michael is saying—and I think he's on to something—is that the only readers we can hope to attract are people who are already interested in environmental magazines. Am I right?"

"Yes! Exactly!"

"So we're competing with other environmental magazines for the readers who are interested in our subject matter. Therefore, a good cover is all the more important because we have to get those readers away from our direct competitors. You see that that's right?" Todd concluded.

Maureen nodded enthusiastically and Roberta looked undecided.

But Nora said, "No. *The Earth's Wife* doesn't exist just to steal readers away from its competitors. We have a mission. Our mission is to encourage everyone—whether they're already environmentalists or not—to live in harmony with the planet."

"The informing-and-changing-opinion mission is so 1960s. It's so old. Nowadays readers are more interested in lifestyles, how they're going to live their lives," Todd said.

"But that's exactly what *The Earth's Wife* does," Nora objected. "It's all about how to live an environmentally sound life."

"He means people want to read about biodegradable fashion and decorating instead of those god-awful stories about farmers contaminating groundwater because they've been using too much fertilizer," Maureen explained enthusiastically.

"Eco-style. It's the next generation of the environmental movement," Todd announced. "The editorial staff has been talking, and we think we should be doing articles on things like how to furnish your living room environmentally and how to buy environmental back-to-school clothes and—"

"Environmental music!" Michael exclaimed.

"That stuff that's supposed to sound like the wind in the rain forest or something?" Walt sneered.

"Actually, I was thinking the Dave Matthews Band," Michael said. "Those guys are supposed to be into saving the planet."

"And what about that guy from U2—Bono?" Todd suggested.

Michael shook his head. "He's only interested in saving poor countries. You know, debt relief?"

"Oh, that's right," Todd said. "Too bad. He would have been worth a cover story. He looks very good on magazine covers."

"Stop everything for a moment. Did anyone read last month's issue of *The Earth's Wife*?" Nora asked.

"Of course."

"I did."

"Me, too."

Michael silently shook his head no.

"You realize it was about just what you're talking about—not Dave Matthews and Bono, but buying things? And how this need for *things* and owning *things* is destroying our world?" Nora said.

"Well, that's one man's opinion," Todd told her.

"But it's been the opinion of this magazine for decades. Even if I didn't believe it myself—and I do—we can't suddenly do an about-face and start telling people they should go out and buy a lot of junk when we've just got through telling them they shouldn't. What about our credibility? Who would believe us when we're contradicting ourselves?"

"Hardly anyone notices that kind of thing," Todd assured her.

I wouldn't, Michael had to admit.

"I don't believe the 'let's change *The Wife* into an advertising supplement' issue is on this week's agenda," Walt complained. "So can we please get back to *your* cover?"

"The Dimauro story isn't about Dimauro himself," Nora pointed out. "It's about how he heats his house with energy generated by wind. Putting him on the cover would be misleading to readers."

"And suggest somehow that we support the cretin's politics," Walt said.

Nora smiled. "We don't want to support cretins, just encourage them to use alternative sources of power."

"People don't want to read about alternative sources of power. They want to read about people who use alternative sources of power in attractive, stylish ways," Todd said.

"Dimauro will be on the cover of this magazine over my dead body," Walt announced.

Todd snatched a copy of *The Earth's Wife* from a stack on a shelf behind Michael and began to furiously thumb through the pages at the front of the issue. He found what he wanted and slammed it down in front of Walt.

"Find me your name on that page. Find me your name on the list of this magazine's staff members," he ordered.

Walt slowly leaned forward so that his bare elbow (he was wearing a worn T-shirt with *Take a Hike!* emblazoned across the chest in faded green letters) rested on the table. "I don't have to have my name on any damn list. Is that clear?"

"No!" Todd answered immediately. "It's not clear!" He looked around at the others. "Am I right? It's not clear?"

Maureen sat perfectly still, her head in mid-nod, the smile that had been on her face earlier now frozen in place. Roberta looked down at her hands and sighed. Michael tried to watch everyone without being obvious about it.

I wonder how they behave at staff meetings when there isn't a stranger at the table, he thought.

"Why don't we vote on the cover issue," Nora suggested.

"What's the point?" Todd groaned. "You and Walt always vote together and Roberta always supports you. You're always going to win. Right? Why waste everyone's time?"

"The democratic process is never a waste of time, Todd," Nora said. "The issue before us is switching to a photo cover. How many people are in favor? Two. Opposed? Three, and the motion doesn't carry. Okay, then. Where are we with the Perkins-Simmons story?"

"It's a story about insulation," Todd complained. "It doesn't matter where we are with it."

"It's a story about a corporation lying to the public when it says the insulation it's selling for use in private homes, office buildings, federal housing—everywhere—is made from recycled materials when it's not," Walt objected.

"Big Business cheating the Little Guy—it's *such* a cliché," Todd said. "We ought to do more unique stories."

"I have this idea for a story about The Body Shop," Maureen explained eagerly. "I thought we could do one about the kinds of people who shop in The Body Shop. We could poll customers at a couple of different stores and find people who buy their loofah sponges and moisturizer there because the store is very environmental. And if we're really lucky, we might find some people with nice-looking houses, and we could do a spread on them and how they buy environmental things and arrange them in their environmental homes."

"Now *that* is what I mean by an eco-style story," Todd said.

"Are you talking about The Body Shop at the mall, where my mother buys that exfoliating stuff for rubbing dead skin off her face?" Michael asked.

"No, no, no. We are not scrapping a hard news story for a photo layout on moisturizer and loofah sponges," Walt shouted.

Todd sighed. "Are you going to do the 'my dead body' routine again?"

"You should probably be careful about that, Walt," Nora advised. "Nobody lives forever. You don't want everyone you know to be eagerly awaiting your passing."

"You're not going to let him do this, are you, Nora?" Walt demanded.

Nora turned to look at Todd. "Investigations into business practices are the kinds of stories this magazine is known for. Those practices affect the average person. We try to be a voice for the average person."

"There are Body Shops in malls all over the country for the average person. Right? How many average people do you suppose know what kind of insulation they have in their houses?" Todd asked.

There are different kinds? Michael thought.

"That's all the more reason to pursue the Perkins-Simmons story. People need to know about insulation," Nora insisted.

I've gone this long without knowing anything about it, Michael reasoned, and I'm just fine.

"Our reporter hasn't even finished his investigation yet. We don't even know how widespread the cheating is at Perkins-Simmons," Nora said. "We're not going to refuse to run a story when we don't even know what the story is."

Todd snorted. " 'Our reporter' manages a Last Stop building-supply store in Indiana. He is *not* a giant in the field of investigative journalism. We really need to be attracting more professional writers."

"Equality of opportunity is very important to *The Wife,*" Nora reminded him. "We don't care who the writers are, just what they have to say and how they say it. And Douglas has written for us before—"

"I did mention that Doug Sinclair manages a Last Stop building-supply store for a living, right?" Todd repeated. "Can't we at least hire people with an educational background remotely close to our field? Sinclair was a pharmacy major in college. And he didn't graduate!"

"But work experience counts," Roberta insisted. "Work experience definitely should count."

"Again, he manages a Last Stop. That is his work experience," Todd said.

"Forget about his day job," Nora ordered. "Douglas Sinclair brought us this story. He found out about what's going on at Perkins-Simmons *because* he works in a building-supply store near the Perkins-Simmons Corporation's home office."

"What if we replaced this story on a company trashing the environment with a story about celebrities trashing the environment?" Todd suggested. "We could do an exposé on who hasn't been recycling her designer clothes, whose private jet doesn't get good gas mileage, and things like that."

"Nora doesn't give a damn about that crap, and she is *The Earth's Wife*," Walt complained. "Where the hell do you get these ideas, anyway? The gas mileage on private jets! People who care about the environment don't have private jets. They use public transportation."

"Thank you, Walt, but I am quite capable of speaking for myself." Nora turned to Todd again. "I don't give a damn about private jets and designer clothes. And while I don't like to think that *The Earth's Wife* is all about me, me, me, I do know that I want to continue work on that Perkins-Simmons article. So we're going to. Once we have a better idea what the story is going to be, we can bring it to a vote, if you'd like, but right now there's nothing to vote on."

"Will you at least consider updating the magazine—somehow, some way, someday?" Todd asked Nora.

"I can consider it—somehow, some way, someday," Nora conceded, not very eagerly.

"The last item on the agenda is mine," Walt announced.

There were several groans and mutters of "I knew it" and "Who else would suggest that?"

"Come on," Walt objected. "We're doing all this renovation downstairs, anyway. The building code says we have to have another bathroom. It's the *perfect* time to install a composting toilet."

"I want to bring this to a vote, and I'm voting with Todd on this one," Roberta announced. "I don't want any part of one of those things. He has my total support."

"All those in favor?" Nora asked.

Instead of answering, people started getting up from the table and leaving.

Michael stood up to follow the others out of the room. Todd stepped back from Maureen, with whom he'd been talking, and signaled to Roberta to follow them. Then he pointed at Michael.

"You had some good ideas, Mike. Very creative. *Very* creative. I think you really understand what I'm trying to do."

Very creative. *Very* creative, Michael repeated to himself. Okay, I'll stay a few more days.

SEVEN

Michael woke up the next morning feeling . . . creative.

His first day of work had gone pretty well. There were all those embarrassing incidents, of course, especially at the staff meeting. But, as his mother always said, no one had ever had to process an insurance claim for a victim who'd died of embarrassment. After all, what was a little embarrassment to a person a managing editor considered creative . . . *very creative?*

I hope someone else heard him say that, Michael thought as he lay in bed Friday morning with his eyes closed. I hope Amber heard him.

He'd slept much better, what with his room being a little cleaner and safer than it had been the first night, and no one had come barging in first thing with a camera flashing and whirring. He pulled on the headset to his CD player and listened to a little Linkin Park while he worked on waking up. When he finally got out of bed and pulled on his watch, he was horrified to see it was nearly ten A.M.

It was nearly ten after ten when he finally came tearing out of the bathroom onto the balcony and ran downstairs, where he found Walt chopping tomatoes.

"Wasn't I supposed to be at work at nine? Or eight-thirty? Or something like that?" he asked.

"I don't know. Were you?"

"When does the office open? Aren't there regular office hours? Nobody said anything yesterday. I should have asked. Why didn't I ask?" Michael demanded of himself.

"Don't be a slave to time, kid," Walt instructed him as he dumped the tomatoes into a kettle. "This hour-and-minute thing—it's all something man has imposed on nature. You should let Mother Earth tell you what time it is. The way she just told you it was time to get up this morning."

"Does Mother Earth know when I'm supposed to be at work?"

Walt rolled his eyes and shook his head. "Listen, kid, I'm going to tell you something important. It doesn't matter how much time you put in on a job, it doesn't matter where you do it, all that matters is that the job gets done and done well. People worry way too much about the first two things and not enough about the third. You got that?"

"When was the last time you worked for someone else?" Michael asked suspiciously.

"I can't remember."

Michael nodded. "That's what I thought. Where's Nora?"

"She went to the office."

Michael groaned and dropped his head onto the counter that separated the kitchen from the dining area.

"She and Roberta had to do the monthly break-of-the-book for one of the upcoming issues," Walt explained defensively. "It doesn't seem as if laying out magazine pages should be that big a job, but the way the two of them carry on about it, you'd think they were creating life in a bottle or something."

Michael lifted his head. "Was I supposed to punch a time clock yesterday? Is that why you're so calm about me being late? You've got a time clock? No? Do we at least fill out a time card? When I worked for my uncle, I filled out a time card."

"Pippy must have been so proud. He always loved keeping track of what other people were doing. He made a time sheet for all the parent volunteers at the cooperative nursery school our kids went to. We had to sign in and out to make sure we were all doing our fair share of the work."

"Poppy," Michael said automatically. "Were there people who didn't want to do their fair share?" He suspected there was at least one.

Walt banged the kettle onto one of the stove's burners. "It was a long time ago. Fix yourself some breakfast. Have what you want. We don't have food rules here."

"What was my father like back in nursery school?" Michael asked as he rummaged through the refrigerator for fruit, which, with green salad, had already made it to the top of his list of least offensive Walt and Nora foods.

"Short." Walt's eyes narrowed. "You know, when your father and uncle would come visit us, we could never get them to turn out the lights when they left a room."

"Oh. Is that all you remember about them?"

"And *you* never turn the lights out when you leave a room."

"Nobody does in my family." Where is he going with this? Michael wondered.

"That's what I'm saying. You, your father, your uncle, Potsy . . . none of you ever turns out a light," Walt complained. "You left the bathroom light on all night last night."

"Poppy."

Dad loved this guy, and all Walt can think of to say about him is that he never turned out the lights? Michael thought.

I'll just say that I'm sorry and that I won't do it again, Michael told himself as he watched Walt shaking his head in disgust as he wiped down the kitchen counters. Then he thought, That's what I should do. Really. But . . .

"What difference does one light make?"

"It's one light in this house, and one light in the house next door, and one light in the house next door to that one," Walt answered. "It all adds up."

"But a lightbulb uses hardly any energy," Michael pointed out. "If every bathroom light on the street were left on, it wouldn't make any difference."

"How much energy does a lightbulb use?" Walt asked. "Tell me that. Well? How much?"

"I don't know," Michael admitted.

"So you don't know that it won't make any difference, do you?" Walt said triumphantly.

"No, actually, I don't."

Michael smiled as he tossed a cantaloupe rind and a pear core into the container for the compost pile.

"How much energy *does* a lightbulb use?" he asked as if he'd suddenly thought of the question as he was about to leave the kitchen.

Walt's body went rigid, and he turned a scowl on Michael.

"Get to work or I'll have you docked an hour's pay," he ordered.

Michael arrived at the office just in time for Annette to teach him how to use the phones so he could cover for her while she went to lunch, which, she made clear, would be an important part of his daily duties. By afternoon he was back in the spare office doing an Internet search for Maureen when he noticed Todd standing in the doorway.

"Oh, To—... Mr. Mylnarski!" he said, startled. Then, seizing the opportunity, he continued. "I'm sorry about this morning—not being here. And about this shirt, too," he said, looking down at the black Limp Bizkit T-shirt he was wearing with a pair of cargo pants, which were sort of dress-up, he thought, since they weren't shorts. "I only have the one dress shirt I wore yesterday. I'll go shopping as soon as I can."

"Don't worry about the shirt," Todd assured him. "Though it doesn't look as if it's all cotton. We prefer natural fibers here. It's hard to iron cotton, but that wrinkled look natural materials have is a message. It says you care about the environment."

A wrinkled look said you were cool, too, Michael knew. The wrinkled off-white shirt Todd had tucked into the top of a pair of perfectly worn khakis said that he was very cool.

"And as far as being late this morning is concerned," Todd

continued, "I know how it is at Nora's place. Do those two even own a clock?"

"I don't know," Michael admitted. "I never thought to look."

"Who would?"

Todd came in and looked at Michael's monitor.

"You having any luck?"

Michael pointed to the printer, where he had made hard copies of news items on environmental issues. Maureen would rewrite them to use as filler on pages that ran short of copy. "I can tell you how many hundreds of gallons of water the average American uses and what's happening at the Department of Energy."

"The DoE's Web site needs more graphics."

"Oh, yeah," Michael agreed. "Way too much text."

"That page they've got on geothermal heat pumps in the Home Consumer section should have something visual, am I right? Something showing, say, an attractive young couple wearing natural fibers, something that will make me jump up and run out to buy a geothermal heat pump."

"Something eco-stylish," Michael suggested.

Todd pointed a finger at him. "Exactly what I was thinking." Then he yawned, stretched, and folded his arms, looking as if he didn't have anything to do. Maybe being a managing editor is something I should look into, Michael thought. I wonder if you need to be able to spell to do it.

"So you don't read many magazines, Mike?" Todd asked.

Michael tried to keep his face from growing red. He'd already said too much about the magazines he read the day before. "Regularly?" he replied, trying to fill time. "I pick up computer magazines sometimes. I'll read under the pictures in *People* if it's just lying around in front of me. I had a subscription to *Rolling Stone* for a while, but I still haven't read the last five issues. I wonder where they are. Anyway, I just buy some rock magazines once in a while now. That's all. Really."

"You're into rock music. When I was your age, I wasn't into music. I was into magazines. The world in magazines was a hundred percent better than the one I was living, studying for biology exams and slogging through *Julius Caesar*."

"You are so right. *Julius Caesar* was one of the most mind-numbing experiences I've had to live through," Michael agreed. "And there seem to have been so many."

"I never thought magazines were mind-numbing, Mike. When I was your age, I loved everything about them, especially the big, glossy ones. I loved the way they looked, the way they felt, the way the pages sounded when you turned them. When my family traveled, I would scour newsstands looking for new magazines I couldn't get at home. While I was in college, I spent hours in the library on the floor with the magazines and journals. That's where I learned what to talk about, to read, to wear, to think. Eco-style could do that for people, too. Eco-style is powerful."

Michael's mind started racing. He hated it when adults started spilling their guts. Except for English teachers, of course. English teachers could go on for most of a class period about their philosophies of life with very little encouragement, and they never put any of it on tests. However, with other people he always had the feeling he was supposed to say something.

He had never actually figured out what that something should be.

Fortunately, Todd didn't wait for any kind of response from Michael.

"It was always my plan to run my own magazine. Do you have a plan, Mike?"

"Not really," he had to admit. "Except that I'm never going to be an orthodontist. Or a dentist. Or anything that involves working with teeth."

"That would seem to leave you a lot of options. That may be a good thing," Todd said thoughtfully. "Because even when you have a plan and you stick to it, it can take years to get what you want." He lowered his voice. "Maybe all those old hippies were right, and it is better to go with the flow. Going with the flow got Walt and Nora a magazine, right? They didn't even particularly want the thing. It wasn't their childhood dream. They never took a single class in communication theory or publication design. They just ended up with *The Wife.*"

Todd wheeled around to look toward the door as someone went past it.

"Nora, is that you?"

"Yes, it is. I'm next door in my office."

"Good. I've been looking for you."

He turned back to Michael. "I'm going to be leaving for the day after I talk with Nora. Would you check my e-mail for me? I'm TM@EarthsWife.com. I've checked it twice today, so there may not be anything at all. If you find a message that doesn't involve me buying something or filling out a survey, send a quick reply saying that I'll get back to them on Monday. Don't mention that I'm leaving work early though, right?

"Nora," Todd was saying out in the hallway while Michael called up the e-mail program. "I have one word for you—advertising."

"*The Earth's Wife* doesn't accept advertising," Nora replied.

"But it should," Todd said as he closed her door.

Todd kept a very clean inbox, Michael noticed. Whatever messages he had received that morning had already been acted upon and either filed or deleted. Michael didn't think the messages he found that afternoon would be kept long, either. Two were offers to provide e-mail marketing and a third was a list of political jokes that were actually rather funny, considering they appeared to have come from Todd's mother. The third came from a Dsinc37 and had as a subject line: Hallucinations.

"Okay!" Michael said out loud as he began to read.

Mr. Mylnarski,

My source at Perkins-Simmons says the health complaints relating to the insulation in question involve hallucinations. There's a possibility that the company has been recycling some sort of material that is prone to fungal growth, which could be responsible for the headaches, light-headedness, and mild hallucinations that customers have been experiencing.

Would you pass this information on to Ms. Blake? Since you've said she is reconsidering her commitment to this story, I think she should know about this. I think it sheds some new light on what we were talking about yesterday.

D. Sinclair

This is about the insulation story from yesterday's meeting! Michael thought. So Todd got Nora to "reconsider her commitment" to the story? Once she finds out about the hallucinations, she'll never give it up. Once Walt finds out about the hallucinations, he'll probably have one.

Michael hit the reply icon. Then he typed, "Your message has been received. You will hear from Mr. Mylnarski on Monday."

He considered his work and shook his head. Too abrupt, he decided. It was true, of course, but he wanted his first business e-mail to be perfect, so he changed the second sentence to "Mr. Mylnarski will get back to you on Monday," which seemed better somehow.

Michael had seen hundreds, maybe thousands, of e-mail messages, and he knew that this one was still missing something. It took only a few seconds for him to realize what it was. He stared at the screen while he considered what he should do. After a few failed attempts, he sighed contentedly as he added

"MPRacine," a more professional version of his usual on-line identity, to the end of the message. Before sending it off, he made a hard copy of his first professional correspondence, folded it up, and put it in his pocket.

I'll give this to my parents, he told himself as he gathered together the materials he'd downloaded for Maureen. They can put it on the refrigerator or in my baby book or something. But maybe I won't give it to them right away. Maybe I'll hold on to it until the next time Eddie farts and gets extra credit for it. Then I'll pull it out so they can see that he may be a big deal in school, but I'm the one who can handle himself out in the real world.

As he entered Maureen's office, he could hear Roberta in her office across the hall, speaking with Annette.

"Oh, Michael! Have I got a job for you!" she called.

Roberta was sitting in front of a large computer monitor. Annette sat on a stool next to a drafting table.

"Any problems with the phones while I was out?" Annette asked.

"Oh, no. It was really easy," Michael assured her. "Not that I want to suggest that your job isn't difficult or anything," he quickly added.

Annette shook her heavily frosted head and dismissed his concern with a snort. "Amber has already told me several times that a monkey can do what I do around here."

"Oh . . . well . . . no . . . I wouldn't . . . say that. Uh . . ." Michael stammered.

"That's just like Amber," Roberta complained. "She has opinions about everything, and they're almost always the kind that will stop a conversation dead."

"It was nice of her to come work here on her day off, though," Michael said. As far as he knew, Amber could be the only woman under thirty-two and a half (his estimate of Maureen's age) he'd meet that summer. He was determined to find something good about her. It was a struggle. "She must . . . uh, work hard?" he guessed.

Roberta laughed. "Oh, yes. She's madly saving for the day she can leave town."

"Does . . . she have . . . a . . . a . . . oh . . . you know . . . a . . ."

"A what?" Roberta asked Michael. "A watch? A dog? An older brother? A birthmark? A—"

"I was going to ask if she has a boyfriend," Michael said. "But if she has any interesting birthmarks, I'd be willing to talk about that instead."

Roberta and Annette exchanged glances.

"She doesn't have a boyfriend because she's afraid that would keep her from leaving town. Not that I can imagine anyone wanting her to stay here," Roberta said.

"She comes from a very odd family," Annette confided.

"*She's* kind of odd," Michael said. "Friendly, but in sort of an unfriendly kind of way."

"You don't want to be friends with anyone from that lot," Annette advised him.

"I've heard she's very unpleasant to her parents. To her mother in particular," Roberta added. "I hate to think what

Amber would have to say about this next job. Thank goodness you're here to do it."

"And it is?" Michael asked, hoping he didn't sound as suspicious as he felt.

"Researching ways to make useful and practical items out of that junk that's stored in your bedroom."

EIGHT

Michael had not been looking forward to the weekend. Saturdays and Sundays with his parents were a deadly routine of picking up the house, shopping for groceries, and running errands, broken up by the occasional visit with relatives (which seemed like running an errand) or hunt for, say, a new shower head (a task his mother and father found so complicated, he had to wonder if they'd really made it through college). These same activities with Walt and Nora would be even worse, Michael assumed, because they would have to be conducted on bicycles.

Then Walt took off late Friday afternoon for a meeting in Burlington with the on-line editor, leaving Michael alone with Nora for dinner. This is not what they mean by Thank God It's Friday, he thought as he watched her poking at a frying pan filled with raw vegetables.

"Where would you go if you could go anywhere?" Nora asked after they were seated together at the table in the dining area.

Michael sighed. "I guess I'd better tell you the truth. I really don't do well with those kinds of questions—What would you do? What do you think? What do you want?"

"What kinds of questions do you do well with?"

"That kind right there isn't good for me, either."

Nora laughed. "I want to go to Iceland. We've got Todd running *The Wife* now, and as soon as the office renovation is done and the new children's magazine is up and running, Walt and I want to take off for a few months and do a tour of places where alternative energy is being used. We could send back stories about them for *The Wife*. It would make a great series, wouldn't it?"

"If you like that kind of thing."

Nora definitely did. She leaned across the table toward Michael, who was trying to pick strands of whole-wheat noodles out from among the undercooked zucchini and summer squash on his plate.

"In Iceland they're working on converting their transportation system to *hydrogen* power," she explained eagerly. "They'll have filling stations where you can buy hydrogen gas to run electric motors in cars. It will be clean. It will be quiet. It will be made from their own natural resources—hydrogen extracted from the steam in their geysers and the water all around them. Imagine that, Michael. An entire country doing something no one else is doing. It will be like stepping into a movie or a book, and in our lifetimes we can do it."

"I usually don't want to do something no one else is doing,

but maybe going to Iceland would be like going into an alternative universe," Michael said. "Which could be really neat. Especially since you could leave whenever you wanted to—or when your vacation was over, whichever came first."

"Yes! Going there would be as close as you could get to being part of a completely different world. Unless you go to the Hebrides Islands, of course. They're supposed to get winds that are sometimes stronger than a hundred miles per hour. There's talk of starting Europe's largest wind farm there."

"Europe has more than one wind farm?" Michael asked. "Who would have thought?"

"We want to go to the Hebrides, too. They're very conveniently located off the coast of Scotland, which might be a nice place to visit even though I'm not aware of anyone doing anything cutting edge environmentally there. Though," Nora added suddenly, "Scotland is famous for its golf courses. I wonder if anyone there is working on an environmentally friendly golf course?"

Michael gave up trying to find anything edible on his plate and wondered how rude it would be for him to root through Nora's kitchen for nourishment in the middle of the night after everyone else was in bed.

"Aren't golf courses already environmentally friendly?" he asked. "You know, green grass and no buildings. And I bet those little golf carts get terrific gas mileage."

Nora rolled her eyes. "Golf courses are ecological disasters—all those chemicals to kill weeds. Plus, they're a terrible drain on the water table. But one of my daughters-in-law plays golf with her parents, and I have a grandson who is on his high school golf team. I could play with them, if I knew how. Golfing is just awful, of course, but my kids and grandchildren don't want to go on wildlife tours with us or visit native craftspeople or travel to the desert to view lunar eclipses. We have nothing to do together. And it's amazing how quickly you run out of small talk about drilling for oil in national parks." She sighed. "We need to do a multigenerational eco-recreation article for *The Wife*. Other people must be having these problems."

No one I know, Michael thought.

"There isn't anyone in your family who wants to take the alternative-energy tour with you? Your kids don't want to visit strange worlds?" he asked. "Because a wind farm has got to be a really strange place."

"Their idea of visiting strange worlds is walking through those foreign pavilions in Epcot at Disney World," Nora said sadly.

"Oh, those *are* good."

A guilty look flashed across Nora's face. "I went golfing while we were on this last vacation. Just once. My son and daughter-in-law took me along when they went to play with her parents. Now, of course, I didn't really know what I was doing because I'd never done it before, but I was surprised by how much I enjoyed it. It was like going for a walk with friends on a nice day, but at the same time playing a game."

"Yeah, I think that's what golf is supposed to be."

"Then we went out to lunch. I wish I could find a golf course with a vegetarian restaurant. At least if there were a restaurant at a golf course that wasn't involved with destroying other life-forms . . . well, maybe that would help to make being there seem less wrong."

Michael stared at her. "Being at a golf course is lame and uncool, but it isn't wrong. Wait. What am I thinking? Of course being lame and uncool is wrong."

Nora gave him a patient smile. "If we want to see changes made in our world, we can't support and use the very things we want to change. What reason would there be to change them?"

Michael shrugged. "Microsoft changes Windows every couple of years even though tens of thousands of people use it just the way it is. And I bet Bill Gates doesn't refuse to use Windows while his employees are working on it."

"I suppose change can come from the inside," Nora said thoughtfully.

"Or not at all, because golf is *just a game.*"

Nora laughed. "Nothing is *just* a game," she said as they got up and started to clear the table together.

After surfing through the six channels Nora's television brought in to one degree or another and finding no nudity on PBS, Michael installed himself on Walt and Nora's computer, where he went onto Instant Messenger and found no one to talk to.

Where is everybody? he wondered as he snuck out to the kitchen after Walt had returned home and headed off to the bedroom with Nora. Bowling? Watching a movie? Sitting around campfires next to lakes or oceans or other bodies of water? At a concert? At a play?

He wouldn't mind if they were at a play, since he couldn't imagine anyone wanting to go to one. He hated them, himself. The one time his mother had dragged him to a ballet, he'd hated that, too. Maybe someone is at a ballet, he thought happily as he washed a couple of peaches and spread some dry, nasty natural peanut butter on some kind of vegetable crackers. Or someone might be sick. That would be okay, too.

The sun poured in the next morning through all the windows on the south side of the house. The light that came in through Michael's open bedroom door improved the atmosphere but didn't make the room bright enough so he could get by without a lamp. Either Walt or Nora had turned on the CD player and KISS came blaring up from the study. It definitely was not what he would have chosen to listen to. But as he finished eating a bowl of dry Kashi (the Healthy Heart System cereal with seven whole grains and sesame, not the Natural Slimming System, which also has seven whole grains, though maybe not the same ones) while sitting on the edge of his bed, the music and the sunlight provided a sort of jump start for his brain. He looked around at the mess that had surrounded him for the past three days and reminded himself that at some point he was going to have to come up with ways to make useful and practical items out of at least some of it.

What, he wondered as he chewed, can you make out of those bleach bottles over there that anyone would ever want?

But Roberta had used the word *research*. Does that mean I'm a researcher? Michael asked himself. Can I call myself a researcher or a research assistant instead of a peon? *Research assistant* sounds a whole lot better than *peon*. If I can find something to make out of those used dishes in the corner in one of the old craft books in the office library, will my name as "research assistant" appear in the magazine? And will the magazine go all over the country? And could I clip a copy of it to my college applications? And would college admissions people then choose me over someone who, say, was a member of the National Honor Society and in *Who's Who Among American High School Students*?

Stranger things have happened, he told himself as he began to sort through boxes of empty, but sticky, wine bottles, stacks of straw baskets, piles of cloth, old clothes, and drawers full of yarn.

An envelope arrived in the mail from his father with a letter that had come to his house after he'd left, along with a check from his mother.

To everybody,

I don't have time to write many letters, and my mother has been up here bugging me twice for not sending her the little postcards she addressed to herself and put in my trunk. (Really, I didn't know they were there for the first two weeks.) So I'm sneaking into the office to photocopy this.

I am busy almost all day. Even the rest period after lunch. I have to play cards with the kids or draw cartoons with them

or do something to keep them quiet. If I'm not doing that dur-
ing rest period, I'm sleeping because after lights out at ten all
us counselors hang around outside talking until way after
midnight and we have to be up at six-thirty.
There are two girl counselors who I've heard like me.

Chris

Michael collapsed against the door frame leading into his
bedroom.

Chris wasn't at a play or a ballet last night, he realized. He
was at art camp, hanging around outside with counselors until
after midnight. Two of them are girl counselors who like him.
And here I am spending Saturday morning cleaning my bedroom. No! I'm spending Saturday morning cleaning someone
else's bedroom.

I've gotta get out of here.

"I've got to get to a bank before they all close at noon," he
announced as he rushed through the house and out the door.
He hopped a bike, worked the pedals as hard as they'd been
worked in many a long year, and braked at stops at the last possible minute so he'd have the satisfaction of making the back
wheel skid and slide. The workout calmed him enough that
when the bank teller announced he couldn't cash his mother's
check or the one Walt had given him for his first two days'
work because he didn't have an account there, he simply told
her to open one for him.

While he was in town, it made excellent sense to find a
place to have an edible lunch. The very rare hamburger on a

lily-white roll with a large side of barbecue chips had a restoring effect. He decided he would try to find the municipal pool because he was beginning to suffer from withdrawal from the one at his grandparents' development. Yes, he thought with satisfaction, swimming is good. I like to swim. I would particularly like to swim if Amber just happened to be doing her lifeguard thing. It would be cool to just sort of run into each other.

The East Branbury Municipal Pool was well hidden, and all Michael got for his afternoon's efforts was a powerful thirst. Soda was another in the long list of things Walt and Nora didn't believe in supporting, so when he happened to pass a 7-Eleven (Thank you, God! A sign of civilization in the Green Mountains!), he pulled in for a Big Gulp.

While he was waiting in line to pay, he started looking at a rack of magazines. That was how he discovered that there was a magazine all about Oprah Winfrey. And what's more, it wasn't a joke. It came out every month.

Why? Michael asked himself as he thumbed through it. He put it back in its spot next to *Martha Stewart Living*. Then he realized what he'd just done. He'd carefully put it back in its place next to *Martha* because all the women's magazines were together. What's more, all the women's magazines with women's names were all in the same place. So were all the car magazines. And all the exercise magazines. Michael smiled and looked over his shoulder to see if anyone was looking. Then he moved the five copies of *Good Housekeeping* to a new spot between *Sports Illustrated* and a stack of fitness magazines. He shifted *Martha Stewart Living* away from *Family Circle* and next to some magazines about bow hunting. He was feeling very creative and reaching for Oprah's magazines so he could slip them into a spot where the guys who read *Car and Driver* would be sure to see them when a little girl pushing her younger sister's stroller hit him from behind, sending him lurching against the magazine rack.

The afternoon was nearly over when he got back and heard old Black Sabbath coming from the backyard.

He found Nora sitting in one of the old wooden lawn chairs arranged on the small island of real lawn kept clear in the middle of the overgrown area behind the house. Her hair was loose around her shoulders and damp. As Michael waded through the hip- and waist-high wild plants that clutched at him as he made his way over to the little piece of cultivated ground in the middle of the jungle, he looked up at the sky. It had been nice all day. He realized Nora must have taken a shower.

"I think Todd has some good points about advertising, Walt. It would make the magazine more secure. It would provide us with some extra income that would mean we could try some new things."

Walt finished changing CDs in the boom box he'd brought out to the table, and then went to stand behind Nora, took a comb from her hand, and began to comb and braid her hair.

"If we're going to start accepting advertising, we'll have to have an advertising staff, and that will cost money. The staff will have to do something to attract advertisers, and that will cost money. We'll have to bring in a lot of advertising to cover the costs of advertising. And then there's the whole issue of whom we'd even want to advertise with us. It couldn't be any company that conducts testing on animals or doesn't recycle or—"

"I know, I know. Still, it might make the magazine stronger and more desirable. Sometimes I think people look at *The Wife* as if it belongs on a table in a museum. Sometimes *I* think it belongs in a museum. I wonder if being more up-to-date would really compromise us that much."

"And how would advertising help to bring us up to date?" Walt asked.

Nora smiled at Michael, recognizing that he was there and had joined them. "I don't know if it would. I'm just thinking about it, that's all—thinking about changing from the inside."

Michael opened one of the magazines he'd brought with him into the backyard. "Advertising could make you look more up-to-date because it would show that you know what kind of perfume and makeup people are using today," he said after he'd found a two-page layout pushing one tube of lipstick. He flipped the pages. "And what kind of refrigerators they're using. Oh, and what kind of ham they're eating," he added, holding up the magazine so Nora could see an unnaturally shaped piece of pork floating in front of a group of laughing teenagers.

"We will *never* accept advertisements for meat," Nora announced. "Never."

"What are you looking at?" Walt demanded. *"Fashion* magazines? Ah, jeez, kid, have I got to take you aside and have a talk with you about what guys your age should be reading?"

Michael threw the two magazines he'd been carrying onto the ground next to Nora's chair. "I'm not sure what they are! And I *had* to buy them because some little brat ran into me in the store and made me spill soda on them."

"Yeah. Sure."

"He's got a couple of copies of *O*, Walt," Nora said as she picked one up off the ground. "My, my. Look at all the shiny pages. I wonder if they use a petroleum- or soy-based ink?"

"There's a question I would never have thought to ask." Michael laughed.

"That's the problem, Michael," Nora exclaimed eagerly. "Hardly anyone does. That would make a good article for *The Wife*, wouldn't it? Something about the environmental impact of magazines?"

"You know, not every little thing that exists or happens has an environmental impact," Michael said.

"Oh, but it does," Nora told him, but before she could get really wound up in what could easily become an essay for a future issue of *The Earth's Wife*, Walt looked up from a page he'd been studying.

"The cover says *O The Oprah Magazine*. Who's Oprah?" he asked. "Is this her on the cover?"

"Oh, come on, Walt. You have to know who Oprah Winfrey is. She has some little television show a lot of people watch," Nora explained.

"*And* she's been in movies, produces television shows, started a book club, has her own TV network, owns a whole bunch of houses, is always on a diet, and runs in marathons. If you got cable, you'd know what was going on in the world," Michael concluded.

" 'Tell Your Story: Speak Up for Yourself; Speak Up for Others; Speak Up for Your Beliefs,' " Nora read from the table of contents. " 'Bathing Suits That Do Your Talking for You.' "

"So is it or isn't it a fashion magazine?" Michael asked. Now that he'd had a few moments to think about it, he thought it might be fun to have Walt try to give him a talk about why guys his age shouldn't be reading magazines devoted to women's clothing.

"It's a lifestyle magazine. Which means it's . . . well . . . about some particular way of life," Nora explained.

"What way of life is this about?" Michael asked. "Oprah's?"

"I guess."

"It does look nice," Michael said, silently comparing it to the newsprint pages of *The Earth's Wife*.

Walt snorted, tossed the magazine onto the table, and went back to work on Nora's hair. "What kind of magazine is designed to tell people how to live? It sounds like something from an old sci-fi novel. The characters in *1984* probably read a lifestyle magazine."

"Walt! *The Earth's Wife* is a lifestyle magazine," Nora told him.

"But *The Wife* is the *correct* lifestyle magazine," Walt explained.

"I see," Nora said.

"I think all magazines tell people how to live," Michael observed. "They tell people what cars to buy, or what exercises to do, or what food to eat, or what politicians to believe. They're all trying to convince their readers of something. You know, Todd says that when he was a teenager, he learned things like what to think and how to dress from magazines. I buy stuff for my computer because I've read about it in a magazine. Computer magazines are for people who use computers. Aren't they lifestyle magazines, too?"

Nora's eyes widened as if Michael had made her consider something that had never occurred to her before. For the first time he noticed their color—a pale shade of blue-gray that he wasn't aware of seeing very often. They were focused totally on him and gave the impression that she was thinking about something very fine and important. Something that had come from him. She didn't look old at that moment, just involved and interested. She beamed at Michael. "You could very well be right. That was very clever."

Michael felt himself blushing. I was right. And clever. And two days ago I was creative. Could I have become smarter the last few days?

Walt broke in on his moment of satisfaction and cut it short. "Getting kind of chummy with Toddy, aren't you? Let me tell you something about Todd."

Michael grinned. "Let" you? he thought. Like I could stop you.

"Todd Mylnarski is a fair-weather environmentalist. He's all for saving the planet so long as it's easy, it's convenient, and it's attractive," Walt complained.

"That doesn't sound so bad," Michael said.

"You'll never see Todd Mylnarski parking his butt on a composting toilet. It's not pretty enough. It's too abnormal. That's how you tell the men from the boys in the environmental movement," Walt went on.

"There are women in the environmental movement, women who are perfectly willing to park their butts on composting toilets," Nora snapped.

"I was speaking metaphorically. You can tell the real environmentalists from the ones who are only into eco-style/eco-chic garbage by things like whether or not they're willing to use a composting toilet. And while we're speaking of eco-style, the important word in that term is *style*. When ecology is no longer in *style*, the Todds of this world won't be having any part of it," Walt said.

"So why did you hire him as your managing editor?" Michael asked.

"We didn't realize how shallow his commitment is," Nora explained. "And we'd never had a managing editor before. Technically, a managing editor should just edit the magazine on a day-to-day basis, so why should he have to share our philosophy?"

"We thought he'd just do his job and not try to change things," Walt said.

"Not that change is necessarily bad," Nora added.

"If it's not broken, don't fix it," Walt insisted as he put a cloth-covered elastic at the end of the long braid he'd made with Nora's hair. "We still have a good circulation. According to the guys at the circulation fulfillment company, we continue to get new subscribers. It isn't just the same people renewing year after year."

"I hope that they're . . . twenty-first century people," Nora said. "Change happens. I hate to feel that we're unwilling to change, to keep up with what's going on in the world. I don't want people to be reading us because they're totally out of what's going on in society, and they turn to us because we're totally out of what's going on in society, too." Nora turned around and looked at her husband. "We used to be cool, Walt."

Michael studied the two elderly people in front of him. They used to be cool?

No way am I going to let that happen to me, he thought. I am never going to become uncool.

"Maybe Todd's right and you should do different types of articles," he suggested. "Stories about insulation, recycling egg cartons, making ink out of soybeans. . . . As a general rule, who wants to read that kind of stuff? Nobody. That's what makes you out of things. If the magazine were more like other magazines—if you guys were more like other people—maybe you'd be cool again. Or at least cooler."

"Do you understand what Todd's really talking about?" Nora asked him. "He's talking about sacrificing principle to sell magazines. That's why I'm hanging on to that insulation story. We have always spoken for the people who are taken advantage of by big corporations. That's a good thing. Isn't it?"

"*The Earth's Wife* is *about* principle, Nora. So long as there is that magazine, there is one person, the Earth's wife, who has a code of behavior that involves taking care of the world in whatever small way she can. You give up that code . . ." Walt shrugged. "There won't be any reason for the magazine to exist."

"But that's what I'm trying to tell you—nobody cares about that code," Michael said. "And there isn't really an Earth's wife. You're just pretending there is."

Walt hit the arm of Nora's chair with the comb he was still holding. "Nora cares, damn it. And you know what? I care. I care about the ink, the egg cartons, whether or not Perkins-Simmons is putting recycled materials in their insulation, all of it. I even care that you left the lights on again this morning."

"I did?"

"Yes!" Walt pointed at Michael and took a step toward him. "You left the house for *hours* and never turned off the lights in your bedroom and your bathroom. What were you doing with the lights on in the middle of the day, anyway?"

Michael couldn't remember. Seeing, maybe?

"I can help pay for the lights," he offered, wondering just how much electricity costs.

Walt threw his hands up in the air. "It's not the money! It's the *principle*. Get it?"

He's really mad, Michael realized. And I wasn't even trying!

"Not really," Michael said, his tone of voice very even, determined not to let Walt know he was shaken.

"The electricity you used can't be replaced," Walt shouted.

"But power plants are making electricity all the time," Michael insisted.

"You're pissing me off again. I thought I told you I didn't like it when you piss me off!" Walt yelled.

"Everything pisses you off!" Michael yelled back. He had to tip his head back in order to look Walt in the eye, the two of them were standing so close to each other.

"That's true, Walt," Nora pointed out.

"Don't keep my lights on anymore!" Walt roared.

"You don't have to worry about me and your lights anymore!" Michael shouted.

Then he turned and stumbled through the unmown grass toward the house, his arms tight against his body, his hands clenched into fists. He was going home. He had the money from the checks he'd cashed. He was going to pack up his things, walk them to town, find the bus station, get himself a ticket, and get the hell out of this place. Nora was easy enough to get along with, but Walt? Michael felt sorry for Todd. He felt sorry for everybody in town.

How much do bus tickets cost? he worried. And when will a bus leave town? It doesn't matter. I'll sit out on the street, waiting as long as it takes.

He stopped at the entrance into the greenhouse and rested his head against the door. I can't go back to school with nothing, he thought frantically. I just can't. This is bad, but going back with nothing when everyone else has been doing all that great stuff is worse. I have to stay here. I have to have this job.

He turned and quickly rushed back out to where Nora was leaning forward, scolding Walt, who had sat down in a chair next to her.

"You only yelled at me because I said nobody cared about your code, and even that's not the real reason you yelled at me. You yelled at me because you were upset because you're afraid Nora's going to change the magazine, and you'd never, ever yell at Nora. Not that I think you should, but you shouldn't yell at me, either," Michael said, all in a rush, afraid that he didn't really sound like someone who was trying to keep his job.

"I wasn't yelling at you!" Walt shouted.

"Yes, you were," Nora told him.

"I was yelling at him about the lights."

"No, you weren't, Walt," Nora said.

"I'll turn off your lights even though it's not going to make one bit of difference," Michael offered. "But it is your house, and I guess that does give you some rights."

Walt looked at him suspiciously. "What rights? Rights as a property owner?"

"Well, yeah."

"What are you saying? That property owners have rights that people who don't own property don't have?" Walt demanded, leaning forward in his chair.

"Are you getting mad about *property rights*?" Michael asked.

Nora picked up a book that had been lying on the grass next to her chair. "Sometimes he's angry, sometimes he's just full of passion," she explained.

Michael looked at her. "How do you tell the difference?"

Nora sighed. "Lots of time you can't."

"Come on, kid. This is important. Do property owners have rights that people who don't own property don't have? Think carefully before you answer," Walt warned.

Michael shrugged his shoulders. "I just don't care."

"Wrong! Wrong answer! 'I don't care' was the worst answer you could give! Not caring . . ."

Michael realized he probably wouldn't have to spend much more time working on his room that day.

NINE

Sunday afternoon, Michael passed on an opportunity to go to Burlington to see a French movie about missionaries in the Amazon jungle and then meet some of Walt's and Nora's friends for dinner at an Indian restaurant. Instead, he biked into town again so he could rent *Lara Croft: Tomb Raider* and buy popcorn and a six-pack of Coke, which he then had to haul back to the house in a backpack and tuck away with all the other stuff piled in his room. The day was made complete that evening when, after sending his family an e-mail, he found Jonathan on Instant Messenger.

MP3: ok i found somebody

ProfBlakie: And you found a computer! In Vermont! When I got your e-mail about the job I thought that was the last communication I'd have with you.

MP3: they have masses of computer equipment here. walt must have bought the first pc ever made and has been upgrading ever since.

ProfBlakie: Like the old Lone Gunman on X-files?

MP3: like the old lone gunman's father.

ProfBlakie: What are you doing?

MP3: talking to you what are you doing?

ProfBlakie: Not much. I have weekends off. For what that's worth. I've done pretty much everything there is to do around here.

MP3: my first Sunday here. done everything by the time I got out of bed this morning

ProfBlakie: Tomorrow I have to sift gravel. Again. It's getting old.

MP3: am doing research tomorrow.

ProfBlakie: Cool.

MP3: i am like a RESEARCH ASSISTANT. sort of.

ProfBlakie: What does a research assistant do?

MP3: research.

ProfBlakie: Of course. Stupid me.

MP3: am researching ways to recycle common household trash into attractive and functional items which will then be photographed and described for article that will appear in The Earth's Wife.

ProfBlakie: Why not just send the stuff to the transfer station like everyone else?

MP3: because we're not lazy and selfish pigs fouling our own living space, the Earth

ProfBlakie: I see.

MP3: have you ever thought about difference between what person wants and what he needs?

ProfBlakie: Of course not.

MP3: we discussed it at dinner last night.

ProfBlakie: We discussed whether the old Charlie's Angels were hotter than the new Charlie's Angels.

MP3: no contest. new charlie's angels much hotter. we roasted hot dogs over fire in backyard. i wanted real hot dogs, but we had hot dogs made out of tofu—which, by the way, stretch when they get hot. point is, i may have WANTED real hot dogs, but only NEEDED food to sustain life and dogs made from tofu met that need. have u ever thought about how if hot dogs are so unnatural because they're made from chemicals and junk, aren't so-called natural hot dogs doubly Unnatural because not real hot dogs? they are artificial hot dogs and hot dogs are artificial meat to begin with so natural dogs are artificial squared?

ProfBlakie: Stop it. You're scaring me.

I'm scaring me, Michael realized. How long have I been here? Four days?

On Monday morning, Roberta asked him, "What kinds of things have you been finding in your room? You said you made a list."

"Butter containers," Michael said. "There are *hundreds* of butter containers under the bed. They're all different sizes and colors and brands. And then there are lots of those artificial-whipped-cream containers."

"Someone must have given Nora those. She would never

buy anything in a plastic container herself. And she wouldn't buy artificial whipped cream no matter what it came in."

"Plus, there are empty bleach bottles all along one wall," Michael said.

Roberta groaned. "I swear, when I was in college, people were making purses out of bleach bottles. Or maybe that was just one of those urban legends, because you never actually saw anyone carrying one of the things. I did know a guy who made himself a vest out of the ring tabs on soda cans, though."

"There are only a half dozen soda cans. I brought them in yesterday," Michael admitted.

"Fortunately that's not enough to make anything out of. Whatever you do, don't buy any more. What else have you got?"

Michael looked at his paper. "There are some used beach towels."

"Are they nice?"

"No."

"Maybe we can make pot holders out of them. What's that you've got written there? 'Blue jeans'? Are there a lot of them?"

Michael nodded. "But they have holes."

"Now those we can use to make a quilt. I've seen a few of those. They're actually attractive."

"A quilt!" Michael repeated. And then he thought, What does she mean by "we"?

He was still worrying about that as he flipped through pages of *1001 Ways to Give New Life to Old Things* (Northampton, Mass.: The Free and Open Press, 1973) at Annette's desk while she was out to lunch. He had already admired the hole cut in the floor to provide access for the interior stairway that would unite all the different *Earth's Wife* offices once the new ones were completed. That meant that while he waited for calls, he had nothing else to do but have his mind boggled by the number of things this book claimed you could make place mats out of—should you want to.

"*The Earth's Wife*," he said eagerly into the receiver when the phone finally rang the first time. "No, but I can take a message. . . . Okay. . . . Okay. . . . You want to know if we're satisfied with our phone service. I'll have to have somebody get back to you."

He took a message for Annette from her son's lawyer and forwarded two calls to Walt, one from the bank and the other from the printer.

"Could I speak with Todd Mylnarski?" the next caller asked.

"I'm sorry, he's not here right now. May I take a message?"

"You know, he's never there when I call. Doesn't that seem a little odd to you?"

"Ah . . . this is only my second day taking care of the phones. I don't know about the other times you tried to reach him, but he's really not here right now."

"Well, then, would you tell him Doug Sinclair called?"

"Oh, hi!" Michael said.

There was a pause.

"Hi?" Doug Sinclair repeated.

"I'm Michael Racine. I read your e-mail Friday. I was the one who replied to it."

"Great! I'm glad I got Mylnarski's assistant."

His assistant? Michael wondered. Who told him I'm Todd's assistant? Not that I don't want to be Todd's assistant, but it's not actually . . .

"It's nearly noon out here, and I haven't heard from him yet, so I thought I'd call and try to speak to him directly," Doug explained.

"It's after noon here. He's gone out to lunch. Would you like him to get back to you?" Michael suggested.

"I'd love to have him get back to me. Do you think you can get him to do that?"

"Uh . . ."

"Could you give him a message?"

"Yes!"

"Would you tell him I'm getting really nervous about the lack of commitment from *The Earth's Wife*. I'm under some pressure here, and I don't want to give in, but if I can't publish, what's the point of continuing with this thing?"

"Just a minute," Michael said. "I'm looking for a piece of paper. Okay. Just give me a couple of seconds to get all that down."

"He'll understand," Doug said while Michael wrote furiously.

"I know," Michael assured him.

"Oh, you're familiar with the story I'm working on?" Doug asked, sounding pleased.

"Sure. I saw the e-mail about the hallucinations, remember? What kind of hallucinations are we talking about, anyway?" Michael asked.

"They involve sounds. People have been hearing things," Doug explained.

"Voices telling them to do stuff?" Michael asked hopefully.

"I wish! There's no way they could keep a lid on that kind of story. No, these hallucinations involve hearing annoying songs. There was one person who would hear Frank Sinatra singing and see all his furniture dance along."

"Wow," Michael said appreciatively. "So people have been seeing things, too. And hearing Frank Sinatra. That's bad."

Doug laughed. "I'd be seeing a doctor if it were happening to me."

"Isn't it funny the way everyone carries on about how awful heavy metal is, and it's *Frank Sinatra* who people hear when they're hallucinating?" Michael asked.

"Ironic, isn't it?"

"This fungal stuff you were talking about last week . . . what does it look like?" Michael asked, settling in for a long talk. "Would it look good in a photograph?"

I'm thinking cover story, he thought. A *photo* cover. With those little things Maureen was talking about . . . cover lines. That's it. Little mini-headlines about what's going on inside the magazine. Something that will make a real impact. Something . . .

"I've never actually seen it," Doug was saying when Michael noticed he had started to answer his question. "We carry the insulation in the store I manage, but whatever it is they're putting in it that encourages the fungus needs moisture and darkness to do its thing. Our storeroom is dry and open.

I found out about the whole thing from the guys who deliver Perkins-Simmons products to us. When they made this huge point of wearing gloves when they were unloading insulation and checking to make sure they were in a well-ventilated place, I began to get suspicious. Then when I started asking the Perkins-Simmons salespeople questions, I could tell right away just from the way they were responding that I was on to something. It seems to be one of those things that everyone over there pretends isn't happening even though everyone knows it is."

"So how big a deal is this? Not that I want to suggest it's *not* a big deal," Michael added quickly. "I'm just wondering."

"If there's something in your home making you sick, you're going to want to get it out of there," Doug told him. "If it's actually in your insulation, you'll have to rip a house apart to get at it. Ripping a house apart and putting it back together costs a fortune."

Michael's mind started going again. Now I'm thinking a *Dateline*–type show with a nice family—a family wearing eco-style clothes!—hallucinating on camera! And Todd would be interviewed about how we covered the story in *The Wife*. And he would mention the magazine's research assistant.

"If any of this can be traced back to Perkins-Simmons, the people there are going to be paying forever for what they've done. They're running sales on contaminated insulation now, trying to unload it as fast as they can. They've got contracts for federal housing. Whatever this thing is, they're spreading it all over the country."

This could end up being a movie, Michael realized. An *Erin Brokovich*–type movie. Except more interesting. Because that movie was really dull. Julia Roberts didn't have all that big a chest, no matter what the magazines said.

"So you'll see that Mylnarski gets the message?" Doug concluded. "And, listen, don't just leave it on his desk or anything. Actually hand it to him, okay? He sometimes doesn't get back to me when I contact him. Maybe it's just a matter of his being too busy or things getting lost or something."

"Okay, I'll hand it to him . . . I'll do it . . . I promise. I'll do it myself," Michael said.

Cripe, I sound just like Amber, he thought as he hung up the phone. She was saying those exact same things to a caller my first day here.

"Todd!" Michael exclaimed twenty minutes later as Todd came through the reception area after returning from lunch. "You'll never guess who called."

Todd grinned. "I'm not supposed to guess. The people who answer the phones are supposed to tell me. That's how the system works. Right?"

"Oh, right. Right. Anyway, Douglas Sinclair called."

Todd's face fell.

"That fungal growth he told you about in his e-mail last week—it causes *hallucinations.*"

Todd jerked his head toward the open library door and led Michael through it, away from the more public area of the offices.

"I've got it all written down here. The hallucinations involve hearing things," Michael said as he read over his notes, "and the fungal growth gets into insulation and is expensive to get out because insulation is everywhere in a house. And the Perkins-Simmons company is pushing contaminated insulation right now. It's running sales trying to get rid of the stuff. Doug wants you to call him. His number is right there."

Michael pointed to the number on the page as he handed it to Todd.

"I made a photocopy of the message for Nora," he added.

Todd quickly looked up at him. "Did you give it to her?"

"I was just going to bring it down to her office."

Todd put his hand out. "I'll take care of it." He smiled again. "That's actually a managing editor's job—to communicate with the publisher. I keep telling Nora we need an organizational chart that would explain the chain of command in this office. Though a pyramid would probably be a better description of how things work around here. Nora is at the top of the pyramid. She's the publisher, and a publisher, being one person, can't do all the work of the magazine. She does just what no one else can do. It's our job to cut down on her workload. We ship a lot of work out—to printers and a company that takes care of subscriptions and mailing out the magazines. They're at the bottom of the pyramid. Then the people who keep the office going are above them. They report to the editorial staff, which is still higher in the pyramid. They report to me. I report to Nora. At each level in the pyramid, we take care of as much work as we can so as little as possible ends up getting to her. She should just be planning and making decisions. She's not supposed to respond to every phone call that comes in."

Michael looked stricken. "I'm sorry. That makes sense. I just didn't think of it."

Todd gave him a little punch. "Don't worry about it. You're here to learn how an office operates—that and to do our grunt work for us. Right?"

He waved the papers he was now holding in front of Michael. "This sounds like a good story. Not necessarily for us, but a good story. Am I right? But here's the thing you have to remember when working with writers: Sometimes it's hard to tell if a story really *is* a story. Is the story supported by the facts or is there another explanation? Some of these untrained freelancers like Doug Sinclair have trouble with that. Doug . . . gets very excited when he thinks he's on to something, but he doesn't have the right background to be able to make good judgments."

Michael could feel his face flushing. Me neither, he thought miserably.

"Don't be embarrassed." Todd lowered his voice and looked over Michael's shoulder to make sure no one could hear him. "You're not the first person Doug has taken in."

"Will you call him back?" Michael asked.

Todd tapped his shoulder with the papers. "I'll take care of it right now," he said as he started to leave the room.

Okay, Michael thought, feeling a little worn out. I've done what I was supposed to do.

"He says he has trouble getting hold of you," Michael continued, his unwillingness to let go of an argument having become such a habit that he automatically persisted in presenting his case even when he had nothing to argue about. "He really wants you to call him back."

"Thank you, Mike," Todd called over his shoulder.

Michael slunk back to Annette's desk to wait for her return. He slipped into the chair and thought about how great it was that people couldn't hear other peoples' thoughts. Because he was really embarrassed about those thoughts he'd been having about the Erin Brokovich movie, and not because Julia Roberts had such undersized hooters. No, it was more that if anyone— anyone at all—knew he'd thought for even a minute that a movie could be made about anything he was involved in, he'd never recover from the humiliation.

TEN

Another twenty-eight hours or so passed without phone calls or e-mails warning of fungal attacks. Michael continued to read and organize e-mails to the magazine. He hunted through old craft books for something he could make out of old shopping bags besides gift wrap or Halloween masks. On Monday evening he brought some of the dishes stacked in his room out to the backyard, and he and Walt tried to break them into small pieces that could be used as mosaic tiles. Their original plan was to use them in a kitchen or bathroom countertop, though by the time it got too dark to work, they had decided to settle on a hot mat for a small teakettle and maybe a tray. Tuesday morning Todd authorized Michael to sign for UPS deliveries, and after lunch Walt came into the office just long enough to sign some checks and give Michael the postcard from Europe his parents had forwarded to him.

MP3,

I think I was in the museum on the other side of this card sometime in the last couple of weeks or so. I can't remember when.

I hate art. I hate history. I hate scenery. I hate foreign food. I hate foreign toilet paper.

I miss <u>Buffy the Vampire Slayer.</u> I miss sleeping late. I miss Dunkin' Donuts. If I stay here much longer, I'll miss my mother.

Marc

Whoa! Missing his mother, Michael thought, shaking his head. I'd have to be in a very bad way before that would happen.

Things aren't so bad, he decided on the ride home from work that afternoon.

In less than a week his endurance on the bicycle had increased to the point where he could stay ahead of Nora, at least in the afternoon when she was tired after a full day of work. So he was the first to see the house as they approached it.

"Someone's pulling into your driveway," he called over his shoulder.

"I think it's Amber," Nora replied.

Oh, great. She's going to see me with this old bicycle helmet on my head, Michael thought. But if he stopped in the street, took it off, and tried to fix his hair, he would look . . . well, that wasn't an option.

Amber was leaning against her car when they turned into the driveway. Michael sped up so he could screech to a halt and tried to whip off his helmet in a manly kind of way while dismounting. He didn't get hurt and Amber didn't laugh, so he felt it was a successful maneuver.

She was wearing a big *Town of East Branbury* T-shirt over a swimsuit, leaving only her legs exposed from the hips down. She didn't look half bad.

"My mother asked me to stop by on my way home from work because she said you had a bag of panty hose for her," Amber explained.

"A bag of panty hose?" Nora repeated.

"Your mother?" Michael asked. The implication of the word "mother" hit Michael a lot faster than that sort of thing usually did. "Ro-Roberta is your mo-mother?"

"You have a problem with that?" Amber asked.

Michael wheeled toward Nora. "Why didn't you tell me?"

"Was I supposed to?"

Michael looked over at Amber.

What did I say about her to Roberta? he wondered frantically. Did I say Amber was strange? Did I say something nasty about her in front of her own mother? Or did I say something to make Roberta think I was interested? Oh, no. I asked her if Amber had a boyfriend. What did Roberta say to Amber? Did Roberta say something that would make her think I'm interested? Am I in trouble?

"Mom said you told her Nora had a bag of old panty hose she could use for stuffing something she's making," Amber said to Michael.

"I know what she's talking about," he said abruptly. "I'll get it. I know right where it is."

He had turned and was bolting toward the house before he'd finished speaking.

Amber followed him all the way to his bedroom. At home,

he had been instructed never to be alone in his bedroom with a girl, which had never been a problem since he had never known any girls who wanted to be in his bedroom, alone with him or not. But here was a girl marching right into what was now his room. Should I stop her? he asked himself. No! Of course not! I'm spontaneous! Nora said so.

"How can you stand it in here with all this?" Amber asked in a low voice.

"This is my research," he explained huffily.

"Call it whatever you want," Amber said.

She picked up a shopping bag filled with gently used gift bags.

"I know they reuse everything for some high, moral purpose, but when they give somebody a nice gift in one of these old bags, it makes them look so cheap. It's the same thing with their yard. They let everything grow up to provide a wildlife habitat, but unless you're Smokey the Bear, it just looks like a vacant lot."

"So that's what they're doing out back. I thought Walt just didn't like to cut the grass."

"Things did work out nicely for him that way, didn't they? He's not like Nora. I think she's just a little bit of a Type A personality," Amber confided. "Not that she's always in a hurry or tense or impatient. But she is a little bit driven, if you know what I mean. She can't let up."

Amber paused, seeming to be waiting for a response, so Michael said, "Is that bad?"

Amber took the bag Michael held out to her. Then she gestured toward the rest of the room's contents. "You tell me."

"Oh, wait. I need one of those," Michael said as he grabbed a pair of panty hose by a toe and pulled it out of the bag.

"Oh, do you?" Amber asked, grinning.

"Were you aware that you can vent your clothes dryer into your house so that the heat the dryer generates isn't wasted by being pumped outdoors?" he asked. "Panty hose can be used as filters for the vents so you aren't filling your house with lint."

"There's a little factoid I can forget immediately," Amber said.

"I want a pair of these things so we can take a picture of one of them on a dryer vent for our article on reusing household items."

"Okay," Amber said as she turned away and started to leave the room.

She was getting away.

"Hey, listen," Michael said as he followed her. "You want to do something?"

Amber stopped suddenly and turned to look at him.

"Okay, we need to get something straight," she said. "I don't date guys."

Michael gasped. A lesbian! I've never met one before! At least, I don't think so. Wait until everyone hears about this. I wonder if there's some way I can send a postcard to Marc. This would cheer him up for sure.

"I'm not a lesbian, if that's what you're thinking," Amber went on.

"Oh."

"I meant I just don't date. And I don't date because I don't want to get involved with anyone from East Branbury. You get involved with someone from your hometown and then you're stuck there or else you're stuck going where he wants to go. I have one more year of high school, four years of college, then a master's program and a Ph.D. program before I can practice psychology. What do you think the chances are of my doing all that if I have a boyfriend back home? Zilch."

She's going to be a senior this year. So she *is* older than I am.

"I'm not from East Branbury," he reminded her.

"Oh. Well. That's a minor point," Amber said quickly.

"And I don't want to be your boyfriend or anything," he added, thinking he sounded very reassuring.

Amber didn't look reassured.

"I thought that was what you wanted—to *not* have a boyfriend," he said as he rushed to follow her along the balcony to the stairs. "Aren't we perfect for each other?"

"What kind of standard for perfection do you have?" Amber snapped over her shoulder.

"I don't know. All I did was ask if you wanted to do something. I'm not interested in going shopping for rings or anything."

Amber stopped. "Oh! Guess what? This is fair week. We could go to the fair tonight."

"A fair?" Michael repeated, not very enthusiastically. "It's not one of those farmer fairs where they always have a country band, is it? That music all sounds alike to me. . . . 'My girl left me, my dog died, my truck broke' with a little yodeling.

And those tractor pulls—they're like watching ice form. Then there's the—"

"You'll pay?" Amber asked.

"Yeah. Sure."

"All right then," Amber said as she started walking again.

Michael followed along behind her, grinning happily. Then a thought occurred to him.

"Hey!" he shouted across the driveway to her. "Can you drive us? I don't have a car."

When he came back into the house, he found Walt and Nora pretending not to have been watching him.

"She's kind of scary, isn't she?" he said to them.

Walt put his arm around Nora's shoulders and gave them a squeeze. "I've always liked that in a woman, myself."

"I've been to fairs before. Really," Michael insisted as he and Amber walked down a path bordered with food booths. "They're a lot like malls. Have you ever noticed that?"

Amber made a big point of not waving to a group of high school students they passed, then stopped and looked at him. "Yes! I have!" she exclaimed.

"You have all these booths and displays where people are selling things like recreational vehicles and cooking utensils, just like you have all those stores in malls," Michael explained.

"Then you have all those places to eat, just like you have places to eat in malls," Amber broke in.

"You have arcade games at fairs just like you have arcades in malls," Michael continued. "*And* you know how fairs have midways with rides? Well, there's a mall in Minnesota that has a Ferris wheel, a roller coaster, a log chute, and a bunch of other things like that. I've been trying to talk my parents into going there for vacation for years. I almost had them convinced last summer, but my brother wanted to go to these reproduction Colonial villages in Virginia because he'd done some project on one in school. Talk about your vacations in hell."

Amber looked thoughtful. "You know, in medieval times fairs were gathering places for recreation and shopping. Malls serve the same purpose today. So you could even say they are contemporary fairs or that they are part of a long tradition that goes back to the Middle Ages."

Jeez, I hope she's not some kind of honor student, Michael thought.

"Walt says he won't go to fairs because he thinks farm animals are stupid," he said. "He says all the animals that allowed themselves to be domesticated are stupid. It's funny he thinks they're stupid since he has such a big thing about not eating them."

"A lot of *people* are stupid, but we don't eat them," Amber pointed out. "Todd would have been brisket years ago if that were the case."

"Todd's not stupid," Michael objected.

"No," Amber agreed. "That was a knee-jerk reaction on my part. I tend to think anyone I don't like is stupid."

"I can understand why Walt doesn't like Todd. Todd wants

to change the magazine—for the better, in my humble opinion, though Walt isn't one to let something like that influence him. But why don't you like him?"

"Because he wants to change the magazine," Amber said simply as they approached the Vermont National Guard's booth. She went up to talk to a recruiter and came back with a couple of camouflage-colored pencils.

"They always have freebies," she explained, pocketing them both herself.

"Why do you care what Todd wants to do with the magazine? I would have thought you'd like the fighting between Walt and Todd and waiting to see who wins the cover argument. You're the one who said I was going to love working at *The Wife* because it was like being with a pack of animals," Michael reminded her. "And sometimes I do feel as if I'm Jane Goodall watching a pack of monkeys."

"Jane Goodall watched chimpanzees, not monkeys. Same order, different family."

"Oh. Well, thanks for straightening that out."

Amber stopped by the pen of a pig that came to the rails beside them and tried to stick his snout out. "If your mother were one of the chimps, you'd feel differently. If Todd gets control of *The Wife,* he's going to cut my mother loose from the ol' chimp community."

"Why do you think he'd do that?"

"Have you heard Todd going on about journalism majors and taking the correct courses yet? Ah, I'm right? Am I right?" Amber asked triumphantly, correctly reading the expression on Michael's face. "Well, my maternal unit has never been near a school of journalism or graphic design or anything like one. She has a B.S. in home economics. She's done freelance photography for local newspapers and *Vermont Life,* but she's never even had a real job with another publication the way Todd and Maureen have."

Amber turned and huffed out of the building.

" 'Home economics'?" Michael repeated as he tagged along after her.

"She went to school back in the Dark Ages when the colleges around here weren't offering the things she was interested in. And she wouldn't leave Vermont to study or work because she was dating my father. And he wouldn't go anywhere because there was absolutely no place in the world suitable for him to start a sporting-goods store other than Main Street, East Branbury. Though why that meant she had to study home economics is beyond me."

"How did she end up at *The Earth's Wife?*" Michael asked.

"She's known Walt and Nora since she was a little kid, which is how she ended up doing a lot of freelance work for the old art director. Then, when the old art director left—and she was old—Nora hired Mom to take the job because she's Nora and she does things like that. But Todd doesn't. And if Todd gets control of the magazine, what happens to my mother? She'll be out on her backside, and she's forty-five years old, and she lives *here,*" Amber said, waving her arms dramatically.

Michael closed his eyes and wished Roberta's backside hadn't come up in the conversation.

"My mother's a lot younger than Nora, and Todd's younger than my mother. Mom owes Nora everything, but she tries to look for ways she can support Todd because—do the math—he's going to end up running the show. Which makes her feel disloyal and guilty. Which makes her a pain in the ass to live with. Not that she wasn't before, of course. Don't get me started on curfews."

"Maybe you're being just a little bit paranoid," Michael suggested, trying to be helpful. "Not that paranoia is a bad thing. I like a good conspiracy, myself."

"If I were being paranoid, I'd believe that *I* was being persecuted. I think my mother's being persecuted. That's entirely different."

That's right, Michael agreed to himself. It's an entirely different category of crazy. One that hasn't been named yet.

"I guess I'm the only person who actually likes Todd," he said.

"Maureen might like him," Amber admitted grudgingly. "She sleeps with him."

Michael's eyes popped. *"They're* the ones who are involved?"

"You've worked there four days, Michael. Haven't you figured out anything?"

"I noticed she always agrees with him, but it's kind of a jump from agreeing with a guy about, say, whether to use glossy paper or newsprint to doing the wild thing with him."

"Todd went mad for Maureen as soon as he found out she used to edit the household tips column for some women's magazine. Last summer, every time I went by her office, he was in there telling her, 'You are *so* creative, so *very* creative.' Of course, I also heard him say that once to the UPS driver when Todd was trying to get him to take a package that was too large. He is a real master of suck-up when he thinks having you on his side will do him some good. Not that he ever sucked up to me, which is another reason I think he's planning to ditch Mom if he gets a chance. If she were important to him, he would have been all over me just to stay in good with her."

"So are you saying that Maureen and the UPS driver aren't creative?" Michael asked.

"I'm saying I wouldn't be patting myself on the back about anything positive Todd Mylnarski said about me. Especially if it were to my face," Amber explained.

Michael sighed.

"Can we talk about something else?" Amber asked.

"Sure. What?"

They looked at each other.

"What's the date?" Michael finally asked. "I think Ozzfest might be playing somewhere."

Amber rolled her eyes. "So what? It's not here."

They walked on in silence for a while.

"Do you remember taking a call from someone named Douglas Sinclair last week when you were filling in for Annette?" Michael finally asked.

"Nope."

"You said he was a psycho! How many psycho calls did you take that day?" Michael demanded.

"Three."

"This one had something to do with threats, and you were supposed to give Todd a message. Ring a bell?"

"Oh, sure."

"Well, what was it about?" Michael asked.

"I don't want to talk about that place anymore."

"Just tell me about the call and then we'll change the subject. What did the guy say?"

"He said he was getting threatening phone calls about the article he was working on. He gave me the name of a company, but I don't remember it."

"Perkins-Simmons?" Michael suggested.

"Remember how I just said I don't remember?"

"Well, what did he say about the calls?" Michael asked, exasperated.

"I told you."

"That's all?"

"If there were more to tell, I'd tell, but there's not. Well, no, I wouldn't tell because I don't want to talk about this anymore. But as it turns out, I have nothing more to say anyway. I believe that's what's known as serendipity," Amber said, looking thoughtful. "You know, when something works out without even trying."

"No, I don't know. It hardly ever happens to me. Do you think Todd did anything about that call?"

"Like what? Oh, look. They've got a Drop of Terror over at the midway this year," Amber said, pointing to something ahead of them. "Let's go take a ride."

"Wait! They've got a Ferris wheel, too. I've got a cell phone." Michael pulled his phone out of one of the pockets of his shorts. "And no roaming charges. You know anybody we could call from the top?"

"I know *lots* of people," Amber replied.

Eleven

Michael returned home from the fair just as Walt and Nora were heading off to bed. That wasn't an event he usually cared about one way or the other, but that night he was grateful. It meant that not only was the computer free, but he would be able to use it in absolute privacy, which he felt he needed for the trip he wanted to take to the Perkins-Simmons home page.

Not that he actually believed any company would say at its professional Web site that it used contaminated materials in its products, materials that could cause consumers to hear Frank Sinatra singing from beyond the grave where he had been for several years. But he'd heard from Amber about what was wrong with Todd. And he'd heard from Todd about what was wrong with Douglas Sinclair. He just wanted some information that didn't involve someone complaining about someone else. Plus, he was a hundred percent certain there were no pyramid explanations for why he shouldn't go to a company home page.

Ninety-five percent certain, actually, which was why he wanted privacy.

After a half an hour of hunting through specifications regarding the length, width, and thickness of insulation, as well as some stuff called R-values and vapor retarders, he finally typed *fungus* into the Keyword Search box and was told that Perkins-Simmons insulation was designed to prevent the growth of it.

So, he thought, if their insulation is designed to *prevent* the growth of fungus, that means that fungus *can* grow in insulation. Because why prevent it if it never happens?

It was the first indication he'd had that what Doug was talking about was at least possible, even if he was an untrained freelancer as Todd said, and Michael was feeling that he'd accomplished something. He deserved a reward—say, an hour or so of playing StarCraft or Half-Life, if only he could still find the games he'd brought in the mess spread throughout his room. But first he checked his e-mail.

The only message was from his family, which was fine, except it was a response to the e-mail he'd sent Sunday night. And his Sunday night e-mail was now embarrassing to recall.

Original message:
From: MP31985@14all.com
To: RacieOnes@14all.com
Date: Sun, 28 July, 20—, 9:08 P.M.
Subject: The new job
Mom&Dad&Eddie,
know you wanted to know whats going on at the wife—
thats what we call the earths wife. the first day I read

e-mails (which poppy says is perfect job for me) and went to staff meeting. had a much better time than i did at staff meeting dad took me to at his office for take a child to work day. those women who work for you are boring. and why dont you let them vote on how to make impressions for retainers or do x-rays? the staff at the wife votes on stuff.

the managing editor called me creative. he had me answer an e-mail for him friday. it was about a story for the wife on fungus in insulation. the fungus is supposed to cause halloocinations. I answered the e-mail creatively. ☺

do you guys know what fungus is?

That's all.

Love mp3

He cringed as he read the word *creative*. And he now thought he should have looked fungus up on-line himself. Asking your mummy and daddy is so lame, he told himself. Besides, they won't know.

From: RacieOnes@14all.com
To: MP31985@14all.com
Date: Tues, 30 July 20—, 10:35 P.M.
Subject: Re: The new job
Mikey,
Fungi are single-celled organisms. (You're supposed to say funji.) Yeast, mold, and mushrooms are all fungis. They're parasites. They live off other things. I think the fungus you're talking about must be mold because The

Learning Channel did a neat show on toxic mold in buildings a couple of weeks ago. Remember? You watched Fear Factor on the other TV? Several kinds of mold grow in buildings. They cause things like regular allergies, nosebleeds, and memory and learning problems. One state has passed a mold bill that sets standards for how much mold is supposed to be in a house. Insurance companies are paying millions of dollars to people with mold damage. Some people are abandoning or burning their houses because they're so full of mold!
Do you think I should bring a combination lock or a padlock to Boy Scout Camp for my trunk?
Eddie

That kid is such a nerd, Michael thought. You have to feel for him.

Then something caught Michael's eye, and he looked more closely at the message.

"Why, the little dickens," he whispered out loud. He sent this at 10:35, but Mom thinks he's in bed reading by 9:30. Way to go, Eddie.

From: MP31985@14all.com
To: RacieOnes@14all.com
Date: Tues, 30 July 20—, 11:47 P.M.
Subject: Re: Re: The new job
I took padlocks to camp a few times & combination locks to camp a few times. lost the keys to padlocks & had to get someone to cut through them with hacksaw. forgot the

combinations to combination locks & had to get someone
to cut through them with hacksaw. so the answer is it
doesn't matter.

surprised Mom didn't know about the toxic mold thing. i
thought she knew about everything insurance companies
paid for.

MP3

DO NOT tell anyone else you watch learning channel

"Gee, I've never seen you go to the office in anything but a
dress," Michael said when Nora came out of the bathroom the
next morning. He looked up from the glass of peach nectar he
was pouring for himself and saw Nora was wearing a pair of
drawstring pants and a sleeveless shirt.

She looked embarrassed.

"It's okay. You look fine. Good, even."

Nora looked over toward the study. Walt was in there com-
pleting a Harris on-line poll, a favorite activity of his since the
polls were almost always about purchasing habits, and he
bought so little, he hoped to somehow wreck the results.

"I'm not going to the office right away," she said nervously.

Michael's mouth dropped. That doesn't sound good, he
thought. What's going on? Does she have to have some dis-
gusting medical test for some horrible disease? Is she in some
kind of trouble? Has she . . .

"I have a golf lesson this morning," Nora confided quietly.
"My first one."

"You're kid—!"

"Shh-shh-shh," Nora hissed, one hand over his mouth. "Walt doesn't know yet. I'm embarrassed to tell him. I had to ask Roberta for a ride to the golf course this morning because I couldn't ask Walt."

"I bet you're sorry you gave up your driver's license now, huh?"

"No, I absolutely am not. Taking golf lessons does not mean I'm changing my whole way of life or what I believe in or . . . or anything at all. It's just a game, a game I can play with my family. Once I know how," Nora said.

"Hey, you don't have to convince me," Michael assured her. They both looked toward the study door.

"He's going to be . . . surprised . . . when I tell him," Nora said. "I'm waiting for the right moment. Not that he'll be angry about it."

"He'll just be full of passion."

"Exactly." Nora laughed.

"Listen to what I heard about fungus last night—The Learning Channel—"

"There's Roberta. Can it wait, Michael?" Nora asked as she headed for the door. "I have that appointment, and I don't want to keep Roberta."

"Oh, yeah. It wasn't much of anything."

Just then Walt shouted, "Hey, kid! I'm going to take the car out to do some errands. You want to go? I'll drop you off at work after."

"Yeah, sure," Michael shouted back.

"Of course, you're going to end up getting into work late if

176

you go with me," Walt warned as he came into the kitchen. "But you can make yourself a little time card and write 'Consulting' in next to the Wednesday morning hours."

"Thanks," Michael said as he went off to brush his teeth.

Walt was sorting laundry when he came back downstairs.

"You got home awfully early last night," he said.

"We both had to work today. We were being responsible."

"That's sad, kid."

"How long did you expect it to take us to look at a bunch of farmers?"

"If you were looking at farmers, you were doing it all wrong. You got any laundry you want done?"

"I'll do it. Where's your laundry room, anyway?"

"Laundry room?" Walt laughed.

"Well, then, where do you keep your washing machine?"

"My washing machine?"

"Come on! You don't have a washing machine?" Michael asked.

"Why would I? That's what Laundromats are for."

"You must not have a dryer, either, then."

"We have a solar dryer."

"Then why don't you have a solar washing machine?"

Walt grinned at him. "A 'solar dryer' is a clothesline. Now, I only go to the Laundromat once a week, so if you have anything you want washed, it has to be done now or you'll be waiting seven days. You can come do it yourself if you're worried about me touching your Spider-Man briefs. And be warned—I don't clean out pockets. I don't want to hear any complaints about your treasures being ruined if you're too lazy to do it yourself."

Michael thought one of his parents had been to a Laundromat a few times, but only to clean his sleeping bag after Boy Scout camp, and then only when it was so foul, they didn't want to put it in their own washer. My mother would have a fit if she knew I was washing my underwear in the same machine strangers had just washed theirs in. It can't possibly be healthy.

But he collected what dirty clothes he could find on the floor of his room and crammed them into a couple of the plastic shopping bags conveniently lying under the little table against the wall.

"What's all this?" Michael asked when he found Walt loading the car with newspapers, magazines, bottles, and cans carefully arranged in separate containers.

"We're going to the transfer station, too. We'll get it all done with one trip."

"Do you go to the transfer station every week?" Michael asked, noticing how full the back of the station wagon was.

"Actually, it's been almost four months this time."

He held up a white kitchen trash bag that was a third full.

"Four months and this is all the nonrecyclable garbage we've generated. It's a record."

"That stuff doesn't look much different from what's up in my bedroom," Michael said, nodding at the back of the car. "How do you decide what goes to the transfer station and what ends up in the bedroom?"

"That's easy. These things are good for nothing."

And how does that make them different from the things in my room? Michael wondered.

By the time they were ready to leave, the back of the station wagon was full of containers for the transfer station, the backseat was full of baskets of dirty clothes for the Laundromat, and Michael was feeling much as he had the first time he left the house on Walt's bike—embarrassed to be seen.

"Doesn't the town pay to have all this picked up at each house?" he asked as they turned away from the main street and drove up past a church on a hill toward a less congested area. He slipped down a little in his seat as they passed three girls loitering on a sidewalk.

"Oh, sure. But how can I be certain those guys will put everything where it's supposed to go at the transfer station? How do I know they won't just throw the plastics in with the cans? Not that we buy much plastic, but what I mean is, those folks who are paid to haul trash never care about it the way you do yourself."

"The ones who haul my trash probably care more."

Walt, it appeared, had friends at the transfer station. His buddies climbed down off the backhoe and came tearing out of a utility shed to shoot the breeze while looking over what he had brought them. The one partially filled trash bag of real garbage provoked an excited series of obscenities that seemed to provide him with a lot of satisfaction.

"There are some people out in the Midwest who claim they

can go all year without using more than two thirty-gallon trash bags, but I think Nora and I could beat them," Walt said enthusiastically as they were driving away.

"Only because you've filled up one of your bedrooms and your cellar with garbage. If you threw that stuff away like you ought to, you'd be creating as much trash as everyone else," Michael added. "And don't think I haven't noticed that you keep sneaking more things up to the bedroom when I'm not looking. I know that copy of *O* I found this morning wasn't there when I moved in. I bought it, remember?"

"The things in your room can all be used again," Walt insisted. "They're valuable."

"Magazines, Walt?"

"There are people who make art out of magazines."

"Who?"

"Hey, one man's trash is another man's treasure."

"Well, if that's true, there's no way of deciding what's valuable and what's not, is there?" Michael demanded.

"Wow, kid. You're getting philosophical on me."

Michael sat back and smiled. "Maybe Nora could write an essay about that for one of her 'The Earth's Wife in the Twenty-First Century' columns."

"Oh, I'm sure she could," Walt agreed as they pulled into a parking space.

The Laundromat was cleaner than Michael had expected and had a well-stocked soda machine. He immediately started feeding it change, silencing Walt's objections by reminding him that, technically, they were still living in a free country and he should be able to do with his seventy-five cents anything he wanted. The whole experience wouldn't have been that bad if Michael hadn't been subjected to a lecture on the benefits of communal ownership.

"Why do people need to own their own washers and dryers?" Walt asked as he sorted darks from lights. "You only use them once in a while. It would be much more efficient for groups to own equipment like that communally. Think of all the natural resources you'd save if fewer washers and dryers were made. And then what the hell do you do with millions of worn-out washers and dryers? Fewer machines, fewer worries. Makes sense, doesn't it? So why don't we do it? Why don't we do it?"

Michael gulped down a mouthful of soda, swallowed a burp, and said, "Beats me."

"We don't own things communally because advertising companies convince us we need all these things in our homes. We're brainwashed. We're a bunch of walking zombies, buying whatever we're told. And Mylnarski wants *The Wife* to start accepting advertising and become part of the conspiracy."

"Why don't you guys just fire Todd?" Michael asked. "Not that I think you should fire him. There's no real reason you should fire him. Except that you don't seem to like him, of course."

Walt didn't look up from what he was doing. "Unfortunately, it's wrong to fire someone just because you don't like him. And it's probably against some law, too."

Michael nodded. "When Poppy was working, he was always complaining about not being able to fire whoever he wanted to."

"I'm not complaining," Walt objected quickly. "I just mentioned it."

"So you'd fire Todd, if you could?"

Walt sighed. "Probably not. He's good at his job. He's good at meeting deadlines, good at editing copy, and good at keeping track of more than one job at a time. Plus, he cleans up well. He's good at representing the magazine, giving speeches and shaking hands. Nora's tired of running *The Wife* by herself."

Michael nodded. "She has things she wants to do."

Walt looked at Michael suspiciously. "Yeah. That's right. So we have to balance that with the fact that Todd's a superficial ass."

He slammed a washer lid down. "You know, of course, that I, a majority shareholder of the business, should not be talking with you, a student intern, about high-level staff members. Not that I give a damn about things like that, but I think I should point it out."

I could know that Todd shed his skin every night and slithered around looking for small children to swallow whole and there'd be some reason why I couldn't talk about it because I'm an intern, Michael realized. Not that I know anything like that about him. Not that I know anything, even.

He looked around. "What if this Laundromat really were communal?" he asked to move them on to another subject. "Who would pay for the building to house the machines? Who would pay for the electricity? Who would pay for the repairs? Who would—"

"God, you're a smart-ass," Walt complained genially as he headed out of the building. "You sound like your poopy with his time sheets, always wanting to know who's going to do what . . . and when . . . and where. Poopy owns his own washing machine, doesn't he? Probably two."

"There's nothing wrong with sounding like Poop . . . Pop . . . my grandfather," Michael responded as he followed Walt out onto the sidewalk. "And why are you always making fun of what we call him? What do your grandchildren call you?"

"Walt, of course. What else would they call me?"

Anything but your first name, Michael thought.

In spite of the fact that he was so much shorter than Walt, he had to slow down so he wouldn't get too far ahead of the older man.

"Why don't you like my grandfather?" Michael asked, curious rather than angry. "Who do you think you are that you can even make fun of his name?"

"Because he sold out, that's why! What did he use his life for? To help others? To make the world a better place? No! He used it to make a lot of money and buy a lot of things. He started out just another farmer's son, and now he likes to pretend he's the head of some blue-blooded Yalie family. *Poppy.*"

"Poppy's father wasn't a farmer. He worked in a mill."

"You always nitpick, kid. It's really annoying. What I'm saying is that your grandfather likes to pretend he's something he's not."

Annoying? Annoying? He's talking about annoying? Michael thought even as his mouth began to form new words.

"It just so happens that my grandfather wanted us to call him Pépé because that was what he called his grandfather. But the oldest grandchild couldn't say Pépé, so we ended up with Poppy. My grandfather *never* gives a thought to pretending to be something he's not. If he did, he'd pretend to be nicer. That's not why you don't like him. You don't like him because he's not like you. And that's the same reason he doesn't like you. Neither one of you cares what the other ended up doing with his life, just that it wasn't what you did."

Walt looked startled, almost as if he'd been hit unexpectedly. He walked along for a while, opening his mouth as if he were about to say something, and then shutting it again when he thought better of it.

Finally, in a calm, conversational tone, he asked, "Who was the first grandchild?"

Michael took a deep breath before he said, "I was."

"And you made 'Poppy' out of 'Pépé'?"

"Actually, I made 'Peepee' out of 'Pépé,' but Poppy didn't like it," Michael admitted.

Walt started laughing hysterically. "You were on his case from the moment you could speak! What is it? Some kind of gift?"

He didn't stop laughing until they were standing in front of the offices of *The Earth's Wife*.

When Walt unlocked the door and let them in to the construction area on the street level, there was no sign of life.

"Ah, damn, look at this!" he complained. "There's no one working in there. I swear, for every day they work, they take off three."

They could hear the sound of voices that seemed to be coming from over their heads. They followed the noise until they were looking up through the hole that had been cut in the floor of the reception area above them.

"Annette!" Walt shouted. "Annette! Hey! Anybody up there!"

Annette hung her head over the side of the hole.

"Be careful," Walt warned. "Has anyone been in to work down here this morning?"

"A couple of the guys came in just long enough to say they're going to be working on a house somewhere today."

Walt's response to that news was loud and unpleasant.

"You know the ductwork they put in yesterday?" Annette continued. "You can sit in the library and hear anything that's being said downstairs. That should be fun once they get to work again."

"I'll call the contractor," Walt promised. "I ought to call the regional office of the Occupational Safety and Health Administration," he told Michael. "I'd hope they'd have something to say about leaving a hole like that in a work area. But I'm afraid they'd shut this project down altogether. If I were ten years younger—oh, maybe fifteen—I would have done this job myself and it would be finished by now."

Michael looked doubtful. "You could have done this?" he asked.

"I built the house."

"You're kidding!"

"Is 'I built the house' funny?"

"It's a house. A whole house. No one just goes out and builds a house by himself."

"I didn't do the plumbing or the electrical work. Just everything else."

"Wow."

Walt shrugged. "I had to. There were only maybe four dozen solar houses in the United States in the early seventies. Nobody around here knew how to build one."

"And you did?"

"I did by the time I was done."

"How long did it take you to finish it?"

Walt looked sheepish. "It's not really finished. I sort of stopped working after three years."

Michael started to move away from below the hole in the ceiling but stopped when he heard the door to the reception area open above him.

"You two are late this morning. Big night?" Annette asked.

"It is entirely a coincidence that we're arriving together," Maureen said huffily.

"Both my kids have tried using the coincidence argument. It doesn't hold up in court, believe me," Annette told her. "Oh, and Todd? Douglas Sinclair called again."

Todd groaned. "Why doesn't he just go away?"

"He asked to speak to Nora, but she isn't here yet," Annette explained. "He was not happy."

Michael couldn't actually see Todd but knew he must be standing close to the hole in the floor, because when he muttered, "We can't have him talking to Nora. We've got to bring this thing to an end," Michael heard every word.

"You know I'll support you, hon," Maureen said in a low voice that carried right down to the first floor.

Michael turned to Walt, eager to catch his reaction to that conversation. But Walt had moved off and was inspecting something in another part of the building.

TWELVE

So Todd wants Nora's job, Todd wants Roberta fired, Todd doesn't get along with Walt, and Todd is "involved" with Maureen. Michael ticked off the items in his mind as he walked down the street in East Branbury late Thursday morning. Todd does it all.

Well, so what? Michael thought. Everybody's on to him. Well, Amber is, anyway. And her mother. And Walt and Nora.

But he kept wondering how much they knew about Doug Sinclair. Did they know Todd didn't want Nora talking to him? Had she ever spoken to him or had Todd, being the managing editor, taken care of that? That first e-mail from Doug that Michael had seen indicated that Todd had told Doug Nora was reconsidering her commitment to the insulation story. But had Nora ever said anything in Michael's presence to suggest that was so? Did she or Walt know about the threats Doug had received? Or wasn't that important? Was Todd right, and Doug, being a pharmacy-school dropout, wasn't competent to make decisions about what was or wasn't a real story?

I'm a kid who's been working at *The Wife* a week today, Michael reasoned. I've only known Walt and Nora for nine days. What's the likelihood that I've found out about something that they don't know about and should know?

Prosecutor (Wears a monocle, a tiny black mustache, and high black boots. May be male or female.): What did you know, Mr. Racine, and when did you know it? When did you know you knew what you knew? When did you know what "what you knew" meant? When did you know knowing the meaning of what you knew meant you should do something? Who did you know who should know what you knew? Did you know if they knew what you knew? Did you know if you should make sure they knew what you knew? Were you afraid of making a mistake by making sure those you know who might or might not have known what you knew or did not know knew it also?

Mr. Racine: Uh . . .

"Is that a Cecile's House of Fabrics bag you've got there?" Amber was suddenly saying right next to him. "What did you buy? Ribbon? Lace? Buttons in the shape of puppies or kittens?"

Michael opened the bag and pulled out a small, evil-looking device. "I had to go in there for a seam ripper," he explained. "Your mother told me to. It's for that project we're doing on recycling household items into stuff like table runners and magazine pouches for armchairs."

"My mother never told *me* to buy a seam ripper when I was at *The Wife*."

I don't imagine she'd trust you with something this sharp, Michael thought.

"You're not working today?" he asked pleasantly.

"It's Thursday again. I have Thursdays off, remember? Last Thursday I was at *The Earth's Wife?*"

"It seems like a month, doesn't it?" Michael observed. "Two and a half weeks, at the very least."

Amber sighed. "I'm glad I ran into you. Actually, I was looking for you. I stopped by the office, and they told me you were here."

He glanced up at Amber, who loomed over him just a bit. She looked a little bit like a stalker, he realized.

"I wanted to tell you that I think we shouldn't see each other anymore."

"What are you talking about? We *don't* see each other."

"And I don't think we should."

"Okay," Michael said.

"Oh, now you're hurt. I'm sorry."

Michael started to laugh. This was fantastic. He had had his first date *and* he was being dumped, which was far less painful than he'd thought it would be.

"You're not going to have some kind of psychotic episode right out here in the street, are you?" Amber asked anxiously.

"I don't know," Michael gasped, unable to stop laughing. "I don't know what a psychotic episode is. Do you?"

Amber frowned. "I was right. We shouldn't have gone out together. As soon as sex comes between a man and a woman, things become awkward."

That sobered Michael up. "What sex? We didn't have sex. I would have known if we had sex."

"Hi, Skip," Amber said to a tiny, stooped man with heavy glasses and a baseball cap who was staring openly at them as he walked past.

"That was my bus driver who just happened to be going by as you were shouting that out," Amber complained. "By sex I did not mean the sexual act . . ."

Michael started walking away at that point.

"I meant sexual politics," Amber continued as she followed him up the street. "I meant the whole heavy dynamic . . ."

"Do you even know what you're talking about half the time?" Michael asked as Amber caught up with him.

"And that's another reason why I think we have no future. I always get the feeling you don't understand me."

"I get that feeling, too."

"Oh, who am I trying to kid? None of this sexual-politics talk is true. Well, it's true, but it's not what's making me do this," Amber said miserably. "I have this terrible fear of intimacy because of what happened to my mother—getting engaged too young and having it warp her whole life. If she loses her job with *The Wife* and ends up taking photos of babies in a store somewhere, I'm really afraid of what it will do to me. *That,*" Amber said, suddenly perking up, "is why this fall I'm applying to colleges as far away from here as I can. I'm getting away from this mess."

They were standing before the front window of an old restaurant. Michael didn't want to start walking again because he was afraid Amber would follow along and keep talking. He was aware that girls were supposed to like discussing private details of their lives, but he had always thought they did it with other girls. Probably none of the girls Amber knows will let her talk to them, which is why she's dumping on me, Michael concluded.

"Well, I guess this is good-bye, then," he said, hoping he didn't sound as if he couldn't wait for her to leave.

"This is the right thing to do," Amber assured him very seriously.

Michael sighed and tried to look sad. He looked over her shoulder as if the sight of her was more than he could bear.

He didn't actually see her walk away because he'd been distracted by something on the other side of the restaurant window. The tall, broad-shouldered figure that had caught his attention had his back toward the street, but there was no mistaking the gray ponytail dangling down his back. A stocky woman in tight black shorts and stockings was facing him. She laughed and gave one of his arms a playful punch. It was a familiar, chummy gesture that Michael didn't like the looks of at all.

He pulled the restaurant door open just enough so he could squeak through. He quietly walked across the thin, shabby rug toward Walt, who was slipping into a booth. Michael was standing next to the table for a few seconds before Walt realized he was there.

Michael hadn't meant to sneak up on him. He hadn't meant to do anything. He was too dazed to mean to do anything. This can't be happening, he told himself. I've never known people who cheated on their wives or husbands. Though there *was* a story about a woman at church . . . and a guy at Mom's office whose wife caught him . . . and that guy at the post office . . . and the President of the United States. . . . But, still, Walt? Walt, who lives a special, better life with Nora?

I can't believe this is happening, he repeated.

Walt jumped when he finally saw Michael looking down at him.

"Damn it! I should have seen this coming," was all he said.

Michael said nothing.

"How did you find me?" Walt asked. His jaw was tight, his voice harsh.

Michael couldn't speak.

"We don't know a soul who has ever even stepped foot in this place. It only takes *you* a week to find it."

Michael silently looked to his left and then his right. Walt was probably right. It was not the grilled-unpopular-vegetables-and-polenta (whatever that was)-over-a-wood-fire–type place he would have figured them for. From the smell of things, he'd guess that most of this establishment's offerings were deep-fried in animal fat. And there seemed to be a dress code. He and Walt were the only two men there without feed-store caps.

Michael took a long, shaky breath. "Nora—"

"Would be very upset with me if she knew about this," Walt broke in. It sounded like a warning.

" 'Upset'?" Michael repeated. " 'Upset'? I think she'd be more than 'upset.' "

Walt considered. "Nah. She knows how I am."

Michael's mouth dropped. "I'm sure she does know how you are," he said. He was finally getting angry. "But she puts up with you anyway, even though she's good, and good to everybody, and does . . . you know . . . good stuff. I don't see how the fact that she knows you *aren't* good will make her feel any better when she finds out about this."

"Oh, okay. I'm being a hypocrite. But it only happens every couple of months. I'm able to manage the rest of the time. And what about you? What are you doing pointing a finger at me when you eat the way you do? You don't think you're being a hypocrite, too?"

The phrase "when you eat the way you do" was quickly processed by Michael's mind. Now he was really shocked. He dropped onto the seat across from Walt.

"You're here to eat *meat,* aren't you?"

"Isn't that what we've been talking about?" Walt asked.

"Actually, I saw a woman pawing your arm and I thought you were meeting her here."

The woman in question came up to the table.

"Does your friend want anything?" she asked Walt.

"Bring him a cheeseburger and some potato chips," Walt said.

"Wait. What's he having?" Michael asked her.

"Baby-back ribs, curly fries, and green salad."

"I'll have that, too, but hold the salad. And he's paying."

The woman nodded and started to leave. Walt stopped her.

"You want a good laugh, Liz? The kid here thought you and I were . . ."

194

He stopped speaking and gave her a wink that contorted one side of his face in a very unattractive manner.

Liz scowled. "That's not funny."

She shuddered and started to walk away.

Walt turned and called after her, "Why would I go out for hamburger when I have steak at home?"

"I like hamburger, Liz!" someone shouted from another booth.

Walt sat back on his seat and looked across the table at Michael.

"Okay, kid. What can I say? Man cannot live by bread alone. He also needs meat."

"If you feel that way, why are you a vegetarian?"

"Because Nora is."

"So you've only eaten meat six times a year for thirty years—"

"Closer to forty-five."

"—because Nora doesn't?"

"It's probably more than six times a year," Walt admitted. "I go to meetings. I see people involved with the publishing house. The on-line editor. Whoever. I go out to lunch with people, one thing leads to another, and the first thing I know, I've eaten chicken cordon bleu. Or a lobster. And whenever I'm with my kids, we . . . well, they always hated the vegetarian thing."

"Why do you live like this, if you don't want to?"

"I *do* want to. Nora *makes* me want to. She makes me want

to live in harmony with the birds and the bunnies, she makes me want to clean the air and the rivers, she makes me—"

"I know how she is," Michael admitted. "But you've lived the way she wants to live for *forty-five years*?"

"It doesn't all go her way," Walt said. "I'm not an easy person to get along with, you know."

"I've noticed."

"She took a big chance on me. I was drunk the first time she saw me. I was so shit-faced, I went into a coffeehouse looking for beer. They had a guy there sitting on a stool, reading poetry, so, as you can imagine, there were lots of empty tables. But I went and plopped myself down next to this woman who was sitting all by herself. She had a black cardigan sweater on that was buttoned all the way up to the neck. Her hair was red—not that orangy red like Bozo the Clown, but a dark, brick color, and it was in this twist along the back of her head. She turned and looked at me, and she didn't seem surprised to see me sitting there. She just smiled."

"Why were you drunk?" Michael asked.

Walt groaned and rolled his eyes. "I knew you were going to ask that. You always zoom in on something insignificant. I don't remember why I was drunk, okay? Wait! Yes, I do! I was drunk because Nora and I were *meant* to meet that night. It was Fate. But since I would never have gone to a poetry reading in a coffeehouse sober, Fate had to make sure I was drunk."

Michael sighed. I want to meet a woman that way, he realized. Except for the poetry. I really don't like poetry. And except for being drunk. I've never been drunk, and what if I were drunk and went to the wrong coffeehouse or the wrong table? But otherwise I'd like everything to be the same.

"Nora's the reason I'm alive today," Walt insisted. "I'm sure of it. Without all the vegetables and the natural vacations and the bicycling, I would have been dead years ago. That's assuming I didn't get pie-eyed and run a car into a tree. Or tick somebody off and get shot. Or end up in jail. Not that jail would necessarily have killed me."

They sat in silence for a few moments, Walt smiling and gazing off into space, Michael scowling and tearing the edges of his white paper place mat into little pieces. The arrival of lunch broke up their meditations.

"I have to ask you something," Michael said before he could start eating.

"You don't *have* to," Walt objected, holding a curly fry between the index finger and thumb of one hand. "You're going to, though."

"You don't believe in any of this stuff—solar power, conserving gas, recycling? You just conserve, recycle ... whatever ... because Nora wants you to?"

"I believe in it," Walt said firmly. "You see, Nora is my conscience. She is the closest thing to a soul I've ever had. And besides, she's still really hot."

Michael picked up his knife and fork.

"I adore that woman. If she goes first, I may end up throwing myself into the grave with her." Walt paused and studied the meat on the end of his fork. "Or I may just go home and eat a cow."

Michael laughed and started to eat.

"So, essentially, you eat meat whenever you get a chance, right?" he said thoughtfully after a moment.

Walt paused in mid-bite. "I don't get many chances," he said before continuing.

"And you lie to Nora about it."

"I don't *lie* to her! I don't offer the information."

"It just so happens that I know about something Nora's doing that she hasn't told you about, either. She's not lying, she's just not offering the information."

"What?" Walt asked, a threatening note in his voice.

"She's learning how to play golf."

"Golf!" Walt roared. "Golf! Do you have any idea the chemicals that are poured onto golf courses to keep that grass looking like that?"

"Nope."

"Golf courses are ecological disasters!"

"That's what I've heard," Michael said calmly. "Though, personally, when I think ecological disaster, I think nuclear power plant meltdown. I don't think golf course."

"There are a lot more golf courses than there are nuclear power plants!"

"Lighten up, Walt."

"You know," Walt said, waving a knife at Michael, "the last week we were on vacation, our son, Tony, took Nora to meet his wife and in-laws at a golf course, and they all went out to lunch afterward. When they got back, all Nora talked about was the good time she had. I *knew* something wasn't right."

"Because she had a good time?"

"You're pissing me off, kid," Walt warned.

"Walt, look at your plate. You're eating something that was once a . . . what are baby-back ribs before they're baby-back ribs?" Michael asked.

Walt looked from his plate to Michael. "I don't know."

"Anyway, whatever it was had to give up its life so you could eat it. What's playing a little golf compared to that?"

Walt groaned. "Golf."

THIRTEEN

Late that night, Michael sat in front of Walt and Nora's computer with a bottle of peach nectar, a half a bowl of un-buttered popcorn, and some raisins.

MP3: so there he is wolfing down whole plate of ribs

ProfBlakie: It's not that funny.

MP3: you weren't there

ProfBlakie: I'm glad.

MP3: you have to know these people

Joker741: has entered the room

MP3: chris!!!! you got our invitation!

Joker741: Yup. camp director has computer & is letting counselors go on-line at night so we don't end up howling naked in woods.

MP3: I'd like to see that

ProfBlakie: Why are you howling?

Joker741: bored. also I'm having nightmares from doing too much macaroni art

ProfBlakie: I wish I were doing macaroni art. Sifting sand is depressing—all the paleos who've been doing it for years are on medication. None of the people running this operation has ever found anything more than a toenail.

Joker741: what's happening? anything happening? anything?

ProfBlakie: No. Nothing. It's dead here, like the dinosaurs.

MP3: something's happening here.

Joker741: what?

ProfBlakie: What?

MP3: I'm not sure. I think managing editor has been keeping something from publisher who is Nora who invited me up here but I may be wrong. He definitely wants to change the magazine around but I think he's right the magazine should be changed except Nora likes it way it is.

Joker741: so what?

MP3: I'm wondering if I should tell Nora or Walt what I know about

ProfBlakie: The interns here are all supposed to keep their mouths shut. There are professors cheating on financial statements and lying about their research, and we're all supposed to pretend we don't notice. And guess what? After a while, we don't!

MP3: in movies kids don't tell things they know and they end up being hacked up by mass murderers or eaten by dinosaurs when if only they'd told they'd still be alive

ProfBlakie: Look around. You're not in a movie.

MP3: so you really know things and haven't told anyone?

ProfBlakie: Of course. We all know things.

Joker741: hey you guys! I know things, too! we have counselors who know how to get into the kitchen at night. you want to know what they do with leftover Jell-O?

ProfBlakie: You artist types are so innocent.

MP3: you're lame that's what you are

The next day was Friday, the second of August, and Michael biked to the office, feeling that he knew how to manage himself in the work world. He could handle things. And it had only taken a little over a week. The rest of the summer would be smooth sailing.

After the second line into the office rang four times in the middle of the morning, he casually picked up the extension in the library.

"*The Earth's Wife*," he said. "I'm sorry, she's on the other line. May I take a message? . . . Oh! Oh! Okay, I'll get her."

He put the phone on hold and ran down to the reception area.

"Annette, your son is on the other line. You'd better pick up."

Annette put her hand over the phone receiver she was holding. "I'm in the middle of something. Tell him to call back."

"He can't. He's at the police station. I'll take care of the call you're working on."

Annette started pushing buttons on her console, and Michael hurried back to the office he'd been working in.

"Hello," he said into the phone, picking up on Annette's

original conversation. "I'm sorry, but our receptionist was called away. Can I help you?"

"Is this Michael . . . somebody?" a voice asked.

"Michael Racine. Yes," Michael said, thinking, Hey! People know who I am!

"Thank God. This is Doug Sinclair. That woman said I couldn't speak to Mylnarski, and I've *got* to."

Michael carried the phone with him out into the hall so he could look down toward the other offices. All the doors were open, and he could hear Todd speaking in Maureen's office.

"Just a moment," Michael said as he put Doug on hold.

He stepped across the hall to Maureen's door.

"Excuse me," he said, after awkwardly waiting a few moments for a break in their conversation, which appeared to be about a place they were going that weekend. "Douglas Sinclair is on the phone for you," he said to Todd.

"Annette is handling that," Todd said.

"She had to take another call," Michael explained.

"You'll need to tell him I'm tied up," Todd told Michael. "We're trying to discourage him from calling." He turned toward Maureen. "Right?"

"But . . . you're not actually tied up, are you?" Michael asked hesitantly.

"Yes, he is." Maureen laughed.

Michael could feel his enthusiasm for work draining out of him as he went back to the phone.

"He can't take a call right now," he said. "But I can take a message."

"Tell him the story I've been working on for him just got me fired from my job!"

"Fired!" Michael repeated.

"I was a manager! Perkins-Simmons pressured our regional people, and they fired me!"

"Are you sure?" Michael asked hesitantly.

"Sure I was fired?" Doug yelled.

"Sure it was because of the story," Michael explained uncomfortably.

"I had a great performance evaluation three weeks ago. Three weeks ago! I got a raise! Then all of a sudden this morning I was fired! No warning, no little talks, no counseling, nothing. We don't let anybody go like that."

"But why would your company care that you're doing a story about Perkins-Simmons?" Michael asked.

"Because my company is Last Stop Building Supplies. They're the biggest distributor of Perkins-Simmons's contaminated insulation in the Midwest. That's how I found out about the contamination in the first place. Last Stop makes big bucks on these things. If this story comes out, not only will Last Stop lose money, it may have to share some sort of liability for what's happened. I'd been warned. I received three calls telling me to mind my own business, but I never suspected they were coming from anyone who could do something like this. And now I've got to know—has this all been for nothing? Are you guys going to publish this story or not?"

"Hold on," Michael said grimly.

He put the call on hold, but instead of simply buzzing

Nora's extension and asking her to take it, he went back out into the hallway because her office was right next door, anyway, and he wanted to try to explain what was going on to her before she picked up.

"Nora, can you take a call?" Michael asked from her doorway. "It's Doug Sinclair."

"Sure," Nora said. She reached for her phone without looking away from her computer screen.

"Mike!" Todd called as he came down the hall toward him. "What's going on?"

"Uh, Nora's going to take a call," Michael responded, sounding as if he'd done something terribly wrong.

"The Sinclair call?" Todd whispered.

Michael nodded, and Todd rushed past him so he could lean into Nora's office.

"I'll take care of that, Nora," he offered genially.

"Oh, that's okay. I don't mind," Nora said as she started to lift the receiver.

"I need to speak with him, anyway," Todd assured her.

"All right."

Michael watched as Nora withdrew her hand and continued with what she'd been doing.

"You and I," Todd said over his shoulder to Michael as he headed off to his office, "are going to have a talk later."

I'm going to lose another job, Michael thought as he crept back to the library. I don't know anyone else who's lost even one, and I just know I'm going for two in the same summer. Work sucks. And I'm supposed to do it for the rest of my life?

• • •

"What's wrong with this place today?" Walt asked after he'd been in the office less than half an hour. "I'm not a particularly sensitive sort of guy, and even I think the atmosphere here is so heavy, I'm afraid I'm going to end up with a sinus headache."

Michael just shrugged on his way out through the reception area. He had been hidden in the library since Todd took Doug Sinclair's call. He had left his door half closed, hoping Todd wouldn't notice him in there, and it seemed to have worked. It was now a little past noon, and he thought he was justified in using lunch as an excuse to escape for a while.

After picking up a roast beef sub, some chips, and a good-sized bottle of Gatorade, he still wasn't ready to face work. There was a small, old-fashioned town green with a few benches, but he didn't want to sit unprotected out in the open. Anyone who was out on his lunch hour taking a stroll on his way to pick up a salad and some fruit juice might see him and decide there was no time like the present to chew him out. So Michael went back to the office, dropped down through the hole for the new stairway, and hid out in the construction site, which was, once again, without a crew. He settled down in a corner. Before he could even get his lunch out of the bag, he heard someone talking nearby. He froze, looked around, and realized the voices were coming from some ductwork in what was going to be the next office.

"What is this?" Walt laughed nastily from somewhere above his head. (The library, Michael thought.) "Some kind of hostile takeover?"

"Not hostile, Walt. We don't mean it to be hostile at all," Roberta replied nervously.

"And it's not a takeover, because we own shares in the magazine. We're owners, too, right?" Todd said. "We can't take over something we technically already have. What we'd like is more of a hand in determining the direction of the magazine. Wasn't that what you had in mind when you decided to make shares in the magazine part of the editorial staff's compensation?"

"What we had in mind was making sure everyone had a stake in the success of the magazine so that Nora and I didn't exploit everyone else. That's not at all the same as letting the magazine be run by a committee," Walt explained.

Michael looked around. There were still no walls up. The sound from upstairs was piped into the whole lower floor. There was no getting away from it. I wouldn't listen if there was any way I could avoid it, he told himself. But since I can't . . .

"We are only asking that you change the tone of the magazine, bring it up to date. We've discussed this before," Maureen reminded everyone.

"I think we're only talking about superficial changes, Nora," Roberta said.

"Eliminating investigative reporting is not a superficial change. Dropping discussion of politics and ideas is not superficial. I'm just not ready to give up on those things," Nora insisted.

"But no one is interested in them anymore," Maureen said.

"No one is interested?" Nora asked. "Or you're not interested?"

"It was a fad, Nora. No one doubts your sincerity for a moment, but for the rest of the world, saving the planet was a fad, a trend. It's just not a priority for average citizens anymore. They've gone on to other things, and we have to, also," Todd said.

"Nora, I want *The Wife* to go on indefinitely," Maureen insisted. "I don't like hearing what Todd has to say, but I think that the change to a more contemporary eco-style magazine will give *The Wife* a longer life."

"But there are lots of decorating magazines of one sort or another," Nora objected. "You make the kind of change you're talking about, and we'll be lost in the crowd. The whole point of *The Earth's Wife* was that the concept of a wife was much more than decorating and shopping. What would be unique about us after you've made us like everyone else?"

"Unique isn't all that desirable," Todd pointed out. "If you can be less unique, more people will be interested in you, and that means more readers. Am I right?"

"And we can still do stories on the environment," Maureen insisted. "We'd just make them more attractive, more arty, more fun—"

"More for the people who feel badly because, though they would like to save the planet, it is so damn hard and they are so damn busy," Walt suggested.

"There are a lot of those folks," Todd said coolly. "And they buy magazines."

"So, you both agree with Todd?" Nora asked Maureen and Roberta.

"Of course they do!" Walt shouted. "Maureen sleeps with him, and Roberta is trying to save her job."

"Walt!" all three of the women upstairs cried.

"Well, it's true," Walt said. "Everyone knows she's sleeping with him. And everyone knows Todd wants to bring in someone else as art director."

"Oh, no," Roberta groaned. "I was hoping I was just being overly sensitive."

"Well, you weren't," Walt assured her.

"I wish this could have been handled in a less confrontational way, but the Perkins-Simmons issue forced us to take some action. If we're going to agree to move the magazine toward a more stylish point of view, running an exposé on construction material is really inappropriate," Todd said, sounding very certain.

"You're talking about throwing away thirty years of work," Nora pointed out. "But . . . I don't know. . . . You all think . . ."

Michael's mouth silently formed around one word. No.

He ran back to the hole from the reception area through which he'd descended and tried to jump up and grab an edge of the floor above him.

What was I thinking of, coming down here? he wailed to himself.

He frantically looked around and found a sawhorse. Once he had it in place and was standing on it, he could actually get his arms onto the carpeted floor of the reception area so that from the shoulders up he stuck out up there while the rest of his body dangled helplessly.

I'm lifting weights when I get home, he promised himself as he struggled and watched Nora come out into the hallway with Roberta holding her right arm, almost supporting her.

"Wait!" he gasped just before he collapsed and disappeared from sight again.

"Don't get too comfortable," Walt told Todd while Michael was turning around in a circle, scanning the half-completed room for something he could use to climb on. "This is nowhere near over."

Todd corrected him. "It's over if Nora says it's over. While you are technically a co-owner of the magazine, we both know that *The Wife* is hers and that you've just been living off her all these years. Right? Don't worry, Walt. This isn't going to change anything for you."

Michael paused and waited. He's going to hit him. Hit him, he silently pleaded. Hit him, hit him, hit him.

But Walt didn't. He just said, "It changes everything for me. You destroy everything she worked for and that definitely changes everything for me."

Oh, damn, Michael thought as he finally dragged over a stepladder, climbed up it, and crawled from the top step onto the floor of the reception area. He got up onto his hands and knees just in time to see Walt following Nora out of the building.

"Did you tell them?" Michael shouted at Todd as he scrambled to his feet. "Did you tell them about the call from Doug Sinclair? You didn't, did you?"

"I took care of that call," Todd said, ignoring Michael's

raised voice and undignified entry into the reception area. "Don't go far, Mike. A little later I'd like to have that little talk with you. We're going to discuss what you'll be doing here the rest of the summer."

He turned and started to walk away.

Michael looked to his left and then to his right. Maureen, Roberta, and Annette were all staring at him. He started to turn so he could take off somewhere, the library, maybe, or outside, anywhere he could find a door to shut between himself and this scene.

But he stopped.

"Did you tell Nora that Doug Sinclair was fired this morning? Did you tell her that the insulation might encourage the growth of toxic mold? Did you tell her about the hallucinations? Did you—"

Todd stopped, too. He turned and gave Michael a kind smile. "I know those things all sound very exciting to a young boy, but this magazine is run by adults, right? We can't waste time and resources chasing down stories just because they'd make a good movie." He held out his arm to Michael. "Come on in my office now, Mike. Let's talk."

Somewhere in Michael's mind a message was registering regarding Todd's shirt. It was very cool, that shirt, with its network of fine, natural wrinkles and cuffs that had been undone and rolled back just perfectly. And Todd's blandly attractive face looked welcoming.

Nonetheless, Michael felt himself seized with a desire to piss the man off.

"You didn't tell them about any of it, did you?" he said. "Everything you say about Doug having poor judgment and there being no real story could be a hundred percent true, but if you kept it from Nora . . ."

He smiled, shrugged, and hurried out of the building so he'd have the last word.

Fourteen

When he caught up with Walt and Nora, they were almost at the bottom of the stairs, near the parking lot.

"What are you doing?" he demanded. "Why are you just walking away like this?"

Nora shook her head.

"You are the *boss*," Michael reminded her.

"Not now, Michael," Nora said, her voice trembling, as they reached the bikes. She stood over hers and hung her head. "I don't think I can get on this thing one more time," she said just before she started to cry.

"All right, baby. It's all right," Walt said as he took her in his arms.

"No, it's not," she sobbed against him. "Nobody cares about the things I believe in. Has anyone ever cared? Have I just been forcing myself on the whole world?"

"If you want to give me your keys, I'll go home and get the car," Michael offered suddenly, thinking he'd stumbled upon something that would enable him to both take care of some of their problem and get him out of an embarrassing scene.

"Yeah. Yeah, kid. That's a good idea," Walt agreed as he fumbled in his pocket.

Even with his improved speed and endurance on a bike, it was nearly twenty minutes before he got back to pick them up—twenty minutes during which he was able to run over and over in his mind what he could say to Nora when he returned.

He would arrive in the little parking lot in a cloud of dust, brakes squealing. He would jump out of the car, run up to Nora, take her hand in both of his and say . . .

That was as far as he could get. The words that might console a person who thought everything she had spent decades working for just didn't matter wouldn't come to him.

Both Walt and Nora were standing by the edge of the parking lot, looking as if they were watching something in the bushes next to the pavement. From the back, they seemed just like any other old couple enjoying the view.

"Would you mind loading the bikes into the back of the car, Michael?" Nora asked as he held the door open for her. "We don't want to have to make a second trip to get them." Then she gave an embarrassed laugh. "I guess it really doesn't matter."

The old bikes could be left by the side of the parking lot indefinitely, Michael knew. You couldn't pay a thief enough to take them. But he helped Walt load them into the back of the car, being careful to do most of the lifting himself. Then he drove everyone home and, since he had Walt's keys, let them into the house.

"You can fire him, can't you?" Michael said abruptly as Nora wearily eased herself into the rocking chair. "That employee-ownership thing doesn't mean people can't be fired, does it?"

"What do you know about that?" Walt demanded.

"I know a lot of stuff, Walt. I just haven't known what to do about it."

"Yes, we can fire him," Walt said.

"I don't want to edit the magazine without a managing editor again," Nora told him. "I want to help with *The Earth's Child*. I want to work with authors for Earth's Publications." She grabbed Walt's hand. "I want to spend more time with the kids. I want to go to Iceland. I want to . . . oh, I'm sorry, Walt, but I want to play golf."

"So get another managing editor," Michael said. "Do you have to play golf right now?"

"Wait a minute, kid. Why are you involved with this conversation?" Walt asked.

"The ductwork. I was downstairs," was all Michael said.

Walt rolled his eyes and swore.

"You can't give up on the Perkins-Simmons story, Nora. You can't let them talk you out of that."

Nora smiled at him gratefully, her eyes red with tears. "It's wonderful to see someone who's still young and idealistic."

"I'm not idealistic. I just think *The Wife* is still your magazine, and you should be able to do whatever you want with it," Michael insisted. "Fire them! Fire them all! Get a whole new staff! Don't just give up because a few people are questioning—"

"Everything she believes in?" Walt suggested grimly.

"I don't want to start over," Nora announced. "Thirty years should have been enough. I am too old and too tired."

"No, you're not! At least, you're not too tired."

"And I most definitely do not want to look like an old fool, pathetically going through some worn-out routine while totally unaware that the world isn't interested anymore." Nora looked over at Walt. "And I don't want to make anyone else look like that," she added, her eyes spilling over with tears. "I'm so sorry, Walt."

"I don't understand this. Haven't you guys always been . . . different?" Michael asked. "All that business about living on a commune and those weird vacations you took—the rest of the world wasn't doing that stuff, right? Aren't you used to looking foolish by now?"

Nora moaned. "Our entire lives, the whole thing—"

"What's your point, kid?" Walt demanded.

"I thought you *believed* in what you were doing."

"My whole life seems so silly now. All of it. Silly."

Michael grabbed both sides of his head and paced back and forth in the room. "You've got to stop thinking about your life for a few minutes," he said while still in that pose. "You have to think about Doug Sinclair's life."

"The Perkins-Simmons writer?" Walt dismissed the subject

with a wave of his hand. "Todd's going to give him a kill fee—some money for having worked on a story that didn't make it into publication."

"That's very nice, I'm sure, but it better be a hell of a lot if it's going to make up for losing his job."

"Oh, no!" Nora cried. "He lost his job? Why?"

"How do you know about this?" Walt asked. "How come you know about everything?"

"I've been taking calls and e-mails from him ever since I started working at *The Wife*. That story was about more than Perkins-Simmons lying about using recycled materials in its insulation. There may be something in that insulation that causes a fungus to grow. Mold's a fungus, you know—"

"We know," Walt snapped.

"Some kinds of molds make people sick. This one is supposed to make people hallucinate. They hear things. If there's mold in a house and it's making people sick, you've got to get it out of there. If it's in the insulation, it's everywhere. It costs a lot of money to remove it. Insurance companies have to pay out claims, and some people are supposed to be burning their houses to get rid of the stuff. So if Perkins-Simmons is selling insulation that grows mold, that's a very big deal."

"How come we didn't know any of this?" Walt asked.

"Todd didn't want to do the story. Doug wanted *The Wife* to give him a stronger commitment about publishing because he was getting threatening phone calls from people pressuring him to stop asking questions. Todd wanted to drop the whole thing, but he couldn't say that until he'd convinced you to give it up. So he just strung Doug along until this morning when Doug was fired from his job. He believes Perkins-Simmons pressured his company to get rid of him."

Walt stirred on his end of the couch. "You've known all this, and you didn't tell anybody?"

Michael's face fell. "I couldn't because *The Wife* is like a pyramid with Nora by herself at the pointy part and the rest of us down toward the bottom at the fat part. She's not supposed to deal with everything. The people in the fat part of the pyramid are."

"I'm not part of any goddamn pyramid!" Walt roared. "Why didn't you tell me? I've worked there all these years without even a stinking job title, and you couldn't have told me?"

"I'm telling you now! Doug Sinclair stuck his neck out for a story for *your* magazine, and now he has no job."

"Losing his job isn't necessarily connected with his story for us," Nora said.

"He had a performance evaluation three weeks ago and got a raise. Then this morning, boom, he's out of there. Todd must have believed there was a connection, because at noon today, before you could find out what happened, wham, he put the pressure on you guys to change the magazine once and for all."

"And why would Last Stop fire a guy for squealing on Perkins-Simmons?" Walt asked eagerly.

"Because Last Stop is a big distributor of Perkins-Simmons products," Michael explained.

"Did you hear that, Nora?" Walt asked.

"I am sorry this man lost his job," Nora said wearily. "We'll pay him more than a kill fee. We'll pay for the story as if we were going to publish it."

"That won't be a whole lot of help! You have the means to defend him in the eyes of the whole world. You can publish that story and make Perkins-Simmons and Last Stop admit what they've done," Michael exclaimed. "Mold is a big deal. It's making people sick. It's costing them money. People are losing their homes because of it. This is something you actually *should* be writing about."

"Michael, we can't help that man. Nobody cares about *The Earth's Wife*. We don't matter anymore," Nora said bitterly.

"So you're going to give up because you're worried about what people think about you? What was important to you, anyway? What you believed in, or what other people thought about you?" Michael asked angrily.

He threw himself down on the couch next to Walt, and the room descended into silence.

Slowly, the sun pouring in through the wall of windows shifted as the afternoon passed. A ray of light fell upon the coffee table, the top of which was covered with two or three inches of magazines, including one of the two copies of *O* soaked with Mountain Dew. Through a faint cloud of dust motes Michael absently read, *Tell Your Story: Speak Up for Yourself; Speak Up for Others; Speak Up for Your Beliefs,* and *Bathing Suits That Do Your Talking for You.* Then he absently read them again. And again.

He slowly leaned forward in his seat and started to speak.

"We need to find a way for Doug Sinclair to tell his story. We need to find someone who will give him a way to get a lot of publicity so everyone will know what he's found out. We need to do something . . . something like getting him on *The Oprah Winfrey Show* so he'll have a big audience."

"*We're* going to get him on *The Oprah Winfrey Show,* huh?" Walt asked.

"I said 'something like' getting him on *The Oprah Winfrey Show.* That's what we have to do. We have to find a place for him to publish the story he's been working on. That's assuming you won't tell Todd he can kiss your backside and publish the story yourself," Michael suggested.

"I sure wish I knew who this Oprah Winfrey is," Walt grumbled.

"It doesn't matter, Walt," Michael said.

"No, it doesn't," Walt agreed. Then he turned to Nora. "Nora, did Billy Upton die?"

"What?"

"Billy Upton—that guy I couldn't stand who worked for *The New York Times.* It seems as if we sent flowers for his wake."

"No, we sent a gift for his youngest son's wedding," Nora told him.

"Good. Someone else must have died. I'm calling *The Times,* Nora. Get yourself ready to do some talking," Walt ordered as he pushed himself up off the couch.

"Give it up, Walt," Nora ordered. "We're not going to play out some romantic, glamorous rescue scheme. Face reality."

"I have *always* been the one who faced reality, Nora. And the reality now is that we're shirking our responsibilities because we're afraid of looking like old fools. Which makes us old fools. Now, you're Nora Blake. Newspapers will give you a couple of inches of column space just because you're still alive. If you want to be more than that, then you'd better start thinking about what you're going to say to Billy Upton."

Michael followed Walt into the study. "Good thing you know somebody at *The New York Times* because, really, we didn't have a chance with the Oprah Winfrey thing."

"We don't have much of a chance with this, either," Walt said in a low voice as he started a computer. "Billy Upton was an ass when he was young, and contrary to what you may have heard, age only aggravates that problem. He's got to be long gone from *The Times*. I guarantee you, they pensioned him off at the very first opportunity. We don't know anybody at *The Times* anymore. I just told Nora that to build up her confidence a bit." Walt found a telephone number in the computer's address book and took a deep breath. "Okay. I can do this. I've done a lot harder things."

"Like what?" Michael asked.

"Never mind," Walt hissed. He stood with his hand on the telephone receiver, trying to collect himself.

"What's the number?" Michael asked, pulling his cell phone from his pocket. "I know how to make a phone call, and I don't get charged roaming rates."

"Ask for Bill Upton," Walt told him as he pointed to the number on the computer monitor. "When they say they have no one working there by that name, ask if they know who re-placed him and tell them to connect you to him. It's the best we can do."

"Oh, shoot. It's one of those automated things where you have to punch in your party's extension," Michael announced.

"Punch in that extension right there," Walt said, pointing to the computer screen again. "It's only about twenty years old."

"Hello?" Michael said into the phone. He cleared his throat. "I'm trying to reach Bill Upton. I'm calling for . . . I got a live person, and he's switching me already. . . . Hello. This is Michael Racine from *The Earth's Wife*. I'm calling for Nora Blake, our publisher. She'd like to speak to Mr. Upton." He covered the receiver with his hand. "Walt! He has his own secre-tary!"

Walt grabbed the phone away from him. "Billy!" he bel-lowed. "It's Walt Marcello. . . . Yeah, that Walt Marcello. How many others are there? . . . Dead? Where did you hear that? . . . You can't remember, huh." Walt turned to Michael and tapped the side of his head. "I'm calling because Nora and I have stum-bled upon a little something we can't use ourselves, and we thought you might be interested. . . . Well, *The Wife* is a monthly, you know, and this is something that ought to hit the streets pretty soon. . . . Just a minute, I'm going to put her on."

Walt wrapped one large hand around the telephone mouth-piece and ran with it out into the other room.

"You were right, Nora, Billy Upton is still alive. And guess what? He's got some kind of big editorial position. What's this world coming to? He's waiting to talk to you."

"No, Walt. We're not going to let this drag on any longer."

Michael ran into the room and stood over Nora's chair. "You're going to make Walt look like a fool, Nora. Don't do that to him. Please."

Nora scowled up at him and slowly got out of her chair. She stood staring at the phone Walt was holding for a second, then she put out her hand to take it.

"Hello, Billy. How are you?" she asked as she walked with the phone against her ear over to the wall of windows and stood in front of it, looking out into the greenhouse. "Has Walt told you much about what we want to speak to you about? . . . Well, it involves the Perkins-Simmons Corporation. . . . That's the one. . . ."

FIFTEEN

I don't feel comfortable changing the covers for *The Earth's Wife* so soon after Todd leaves," Nora said two Fridays later.

She was one of a group gathered behind Roberta's chair late in the afternoon while Roberta moved various outlines around on the computer screen in her office and experimented with different fonts.

"It's not as if he died," Michael pointed out.

"No, the SOB had been sending out résumés behind our backs all summer, and when we told him he couldn't have his own way, he went to another magazine without even giving us two weeks' notice," Walt agreed. "I *wish* he'd died."

"But don't you feel that making a change he was so interested in when he's only been gone a few days is taking advantage of Todd's personal creative property?" Nora asked.

" 'Creative property'?" Michael repeated.

"This particular cover is Michael's idea, not Todd's, so it's Michael's creative property," Roberta said. "I'll have it up in a minute."

" 'Creative property'?" Michael repeated again.

"Perhaps creativity is something no one can own," Nora said thoughtfully. "I wonder if we've ever done an essay on that for *The Wife*? Hmmm."

"I love it when she talks like that," Walt whispered near Michael's ear.

"You don't think she's kind of scary?" Michael asked in a low voice.

"Oh, yeah!"

"It's going to be months before we can have a new cover on the magazine. It will be fine," Roberta assured Nora.

"I wish you'd had that last meeting with Todd in the library. I could have just accidentally been downstairs and heard the whole thing through the ductwork," Michael said while Roberta continued to work at her keyboard.

"Come on, kid. You can't tell an employee to kiss your ass in a public room. It's got to be done in a private office. Some things are just plain wrong," Walt explained. "I wish we'd fired him."

"He was prepared to continue going on and on about how outdated I am until I handed him that copy of the e-mail you answered for him. It was a pretty strong indication that he'd been lying to Doug about my intentions regarding the Perkins-Simmons story and keeping information from me," Nora said. "And that sort of thing is much worse than being outdated."

"Whatever made you think to keep a copy of that e-mail?" Walt asked. "I almost always forget to make copies of correspondence. And when I do remember, I lose them."

"Oh, well . . ." Michael said vaguely, not willing to admit he'd saved the e-mail to give his mommy.

"Too bad you forgot to take it out of your pocket before you washed your pants," Roberta said.

"That's probably the only reason I was able to find it again," Michael admitted. "If I'd put it anywhere else, who knows where it would have been when you needed it?"

"It was still readable. Todd knew what it meant when he saw it," Nora recalled. "Once he realized we knew what he'd been doing, he went right to his office and started making calls. A few days later he had that job offer from *Cooking Organic*."

"He was so happy when he left here," Walt said. "It made me want to puke."

"It doesn't seem right," Michael agreed. "He caused trouble here, and now he goes on to a job with a nice, glossy magazine that does just the kind of eco-stylish stuff he wanted to do anyway. It's like he was rewarded."

"I don't have any hard feelings. Not many, anyway," Nora said. "You know what I think we should do, Walt? I think we should call the editor at *Cooking Organic* and give Todd a sort of reference."

"*Offer* a reference to that snot when he didn't even ask for one? And he already has the job? I'm not lifting a finger for him. Nothing. Nada. It's going to be all I can do to sign his last paycheck and see it gets mailed to him," Walt complained.

Nora smiled. "Maybe calling his new editor and letting her or him know about Todd's capabilities would be the right thing to do. Maybe we have a responsibility to tell what we know."

Walt started to laugh. "I want to call! Let me do it!"

Nora sobered up. "Or would we just be taking revenge? It's so hard to decide what's the right thing to do."

"I *know*," Michael said.

Nora put an arm around his shoulders and gave him a squeeze. "You poor thing."

He let his head rest against her for just a moment.

"Okay, I'm ready. What do you think?" Roberta asked.

They silently studied the picture on her monitor. In it Nora sat on Walt's rocker in their greenhouse with a patchwork-quilt top that Cecile of Cecile's House of Fabrics had quickly pieced together from the old blue jeans saved in Michael's bedroom. Nora was holding a couple of pot holders made from the old beach towels, and at her feet were the trivet and tray Michael and Walt had made from the old dishes they had managed to break into tile-size pieces.

"Oh, no! That's why you wanted to take that picture?" Nora exclaimed.

"What do you think?" Michael asked eagerly. "Well, come on! You don't like it?" he said when there wasn't an immediate response.

"It's a flattering picture of me," Nora admitted.

"Roberta used her airbrush," Michael explained. "She made you look sixty-five again."

"That was very nice of her, seeing as I'm only sixty-four."

"You guys don't get it, do you? Nora's the Earth's Wife," Michael explained. "If the magazine *The Earth's Wife* is about taking care of the earth, but people like to read about other *people,* then why not put a *person* on the cover who takes care of the earth? The Earth's Wife. You'll be making her real instead of pretend. You'll be able to write about saving the earth, which is what you want to do, and your readers will be able to read about a person, which is what they want to do. Everybody wins."

"You are the Earth's Wife, Nora," Walt admitted.

"You're not talking about putting me on the cover every month, are you?" Nora asked, sounding horrified.

"Why not? Oprah's on the cover of all her magazines. And there's another woman who used to be a talk-show host . . . uh . . . Rosie O'Donnell! She had a magazine for a while, and she was usually on the cover. So were the Olsen twins," Michael said.

"The Olsen twins?" Walt repeated.

"They're these two *really* good-looking teenage girls. When they were little, they were on this sitcom, but they were never both on at the same time because they both played the same part. They're blond and they had their own magazine but it folded. An awful lot of new magazines don't last long. The failure rate is huge. Why are you laughing? It's true."

"*We* know it's true," Walt told him. "We just didn't know *you* knew."

"I know lots of stuff," Michael said defensively. "And I know a lot of people have been on the covers of their magazines."

"All you're doing, Nora, is giving *The Earth's Wife* a face, making people feel that it's about somebody," Roberta said.

"I'm sorry, we cannot possibly put me on the cover of this magazine month after month. It's just too . . ." Suddenly, Nora's eyebrows shot up. "But you know what we *could* do? We could put a *different* person on the cover every month. Because the world is full of people who are taking care of the earth— who are Earth's Wives. And then we can do a story about the person on that month's cover. Yes! Roberta, we need to go through our back issues for ideas. And Walt, what do you think of contacting environmental organizations so they can suggest cover subjects? It's going to take a while to get some covers lined up . . . and find photographers . . . I wonder if we should think about hiring a staff writer?"

Nora rushed out of the room, and Walt and Michael followed her to the library. On the way they passed Maureen's office. Through the open door they could hear her sniffing.

"I don't know if her romance with Todd is going to survive his leaving town," Nora whispered as she studied boxes of back issues of *The Earth's Wife* stored on the shelves lining one of the walls. "She is very upset."

"Ah, she'll meet somebody else," Walt said as he poked at a collection of newspapers carrying stories about the Perkins-Simmons scandal spread across the table.

"Annette says the UPS driver is interested in her," Michael said.

Walt looked at him. "You really do know lots of stuff, don't you?"

Michael grinned. "I told you so."

"Todd leaving isn't a hundred percent good news for us, either, you know," Nora pointed out, suddenly sounding less enthusiastic. "He did a lot of work here. We don't have a staff in place yet for the children's magazine. How are we going to be able to do everything that needs to be done?"

"You can hire another managing editor," Michael told her.

"It will take time to find somebody," Nora argued.

"Especially somebody who is 'one of us,' if you know what I mean," Walt agreed.

"I'll help. I don't start school until the end of the month. That means I can stay two more weeks. There are all kinds of things I can take care of for you," Michael offered. Including, he thought, emptying out my bedroom once and for all and maybe mowing that ugly lawn.

He looked at his watch. "You two have to get out of here. You're supposed to be at the golf course in twenty minutes."

Nora clapped her hands. "That's right." She laughed as she hurried out of the room.

"Thanks for taking care of *that,* kid," Walt grumbled. Then he cringed and said, "Your pop-pop plays golf, doesn't he?"

"Actually, he thinks golf is just glorified croquet. He's a tennis man."

Walt groaned and headed for the door.

"I'll meet you by the car, Nora," he called down the hall. "I'm going to lock up downstairs. Hey, Amber."

Amber, who'd been walking down the hall on her way to her mother's office, paused at the library door after greeting

Walt on his way out. She was wearing her lifeguard outfit again, one of her more flattering outfits.

"Is this great or what?" she asked Michael enthusiastically. "My mother is so happy. My whole life has changed."

"Does this mean you won't be applying to colleges as far from here as you can?" Michael asked.

"Of course I will. My life changed, I didn't go crazy."

"It's hard to imagine you crazy," Michael said. Or crazi*er*.

"So, is it true you were the one who got Walt and Nora to go to *The New York Times* with this insulation story?" Amber asked.

Michael nodded. "I actually dialed *The New York Times'* telephone number. On my cell phone. I spoke to a secretary there, too. I'm also the one who suggested to Walt that he tell Todd to kiss his ass."

"Walt couldn't think of that himself?"

"I thought of it first. I don't suppose you heard that Todd once told me I was creative?"

"Ha! He told the UPS driver—"

"Yeah, yeah, I know," Michael broke in.

"Do you think you're going to be in a big hurry to get back home when your job here ends?" Amber asked.

"Absolutely. I miss cable. I miss DVD. I miss the twenty-first century."

"You wouldn't consider hanging around East Branbury or coming up here during the school year to bother someone you'd been dating over the summer?" she continued.

"Never."

"Well, then, we could go to a movie this weekend," Amber offered.

"You have movies here, huh? Talkies, or does someone sit down in front and play the piano?"

"I'll drive, but you'll have to pay."

"Oh, all right," Michael agreed after just the right amount of hesitation. "But I'm not going to go see anything foreign or anything about people dying or—"

Amber smiled. "I'm here to pick up my mother, so I've got to go now. I'll call you at Walt and Nora's and let you know what we're going to see."

She is *so* scary, Michael thought as she walked away.

He had just started to fold up the newspapers spread across the library table when the headline *Vermont Publication Involved With Perkins-Simmons Decision to Withdraw Products* in a local paper caught his eye.

> The Perkins-Simmons Corporation confirmed today that the company has withdrawn three lines of its best-selling insulation after allegations that the products were an agent for a fungus associated with headaches and hallucinations were made public last week. The company was forced into the action after *The New York Times* published an article claiming Perkins-Simmons was being investigated by both the Occupational Safety and Health Administration (OSHA) and the Center for Disease Control (CDC). *The Times* broke the story after

being contacted by Nora Blake of *The Earth's Wife,* the monthly environmental journal with home offices in East Branbury. Blake and her husband, Walt Marcello, founded and own *The Earth's Wife,* which has been a Vermont institution for over three decades.

The article included a picture of the Perkins-Simmons national headquarters and an old file photo. In it two people stood in front of a messy desk. The woman was leaning against it and facing forward. Two long, dark braids hung down either side of her head almost to the top of her tight blue jeans. She looked very serious. An enormous, solid-looking man with a dark ponytail stood next to her. He was facing her, but his head was turned just enough so he could look at the camera. A sly smile twisted his mouth.

Michael reached out and touched the picture. You guys *were* cool, he was thinking when he was interrupted by a long stream of profanities floating up through the ductwork from the construction area below.

"The contractor was using Perkins-Simmons insulation!" Walt roared. "He's going to have to tear it all out and start over. I'm not going to live long enough to see this job finished!"

Michael laughed and left the room.

Then he came back so he could turn out the light.